I0670550

The
Link

Taurus King

ISBN-13: 978-0615980799

DEDICATION

Dedicated to my wonderful family. My wife Kendi and three beautiful daughters Alexis, Lauren and Rylie. My mother Sarah, mother-in-love Gail, Pappa T and brother Adrian. My aunts, uncles and a host of cousins. Thanks for your support and always believing in me. Thanks to my circle of friends. Each of you are an inspiration to me as you aspire to be better and greater.

CONTENTS

ACKNOWLEDGMENTS

I'd like to say thank you to Gloria Marie, Frederick Johnson, Secret Entourage, Anne Seebaldt, Richard Branson, Ricardo Miller, Steve Harvey, TD Jakes and Pastor Danny Wegman.

1 CHAPTER
RUDE AWAKENING

It's two in the morning at the Rivers' Farm in Red Back, Louisiana and eight-year-old Sidney Rivers wakes up to use the bathroom. As he walks down the hallway, he passes his mother Marcy's room and it's dark and empty, since she works at night. On the right is Aunt Earnestine's room, which is also dark but filled with her loud snoring coming from under the door. Sidney is still half asleep as he walks in his green "Incredible Hulk" pajamas toward the bathroom, which has a light on with the door closed. It's probably his uncle Ray in there. As he gets closer to knock on the door he's startled as he bumps into a lady wearing nothing but a white bra and panties.

"And what is your name, Cutie Pie?" she asks while whispering with a smell of intoxication.
This beautiful, attractive woman kneels down to Sidney's level and rubs his head.

"Ray didn't tell me he had a cute little brother," she tells him in a deep southern drawl.

It's one of Uncle Ray's girlfriends. He snuck her in while everyone else was asleep. Ray comes out of the bathroom and his eyes get big at what he sees.

"What are you doing out in the hallway," he whispers with excitement in his voice. "I told you to stay in my room!"

"Wait a minute," she says loudly. "You don't own me!"

She's waking up the rest of the household, including Aunt Earnestine and, more importantly, Grandma Betty and Grandpa Charlie downstairs.

"Who is making all that racket up there at 2:00 in the morning?" says a loud voice coming from downstairs.

It's Grandma Betty and she wants to know what's going on upstairs in her house.

"Ohhhh, God, this is not happening," says Ray, as he knows all hell will break loose when his parents find out he snuck a woman into their house in the early morning hours.

"Nothing, Momma, it's just Earnestine sleep-walking," says Ray as he yells downstairs.

A door creaks open. It's Aunt Earnestine, who's been awakened by the commotion.

"Ray! Why is Trina Murphy standing half-naked in front of our nephew?" she asks, puzzled. She quickly grabs Sidney and covers his eyes.

"You are such an idiot," she says, shaking her head.

By this time, Grandma and Grandpa are halfway upstairs. They're in their early fifties, but they're moving up the stairs in a hurry to see what's going on. When they finally make it to the top, Aunt Earnestine tells them about Ray's secret visitor.

"Boy, have you lost your mind?" asks grandpa as he shakes his head and looks at Ray in great disappointment.

"Baby maybe you should put some clothes on and go on home." Grandma Betty says to the lady who is still standing half naked in the hallway with no sense of shame.

"Well ma'am, Ray usually lets me spend the night." says the drunk lady with an alcoholic slur.

"What?" replies Grandma with a sense of shock. The news makes her knees get weak as she holds on to a table in the hallway. She can't believe a lady who she's never met, has been spending nights upstairs in her house.

"Oh God this can't be happening to me!" Ray says.

"Oh no... no... no! I'm telling it all since you so ashamed of me...Ray!" The drunk lady says as she continues to expose Ray's secret of sneaking her in late at night.

"Ray get her out of here now!" Grandpa Charlie screams.

****

By this time, the sun has risen. Marcy, Sidney's mom, is coming home after working the night shift at the hospital. She works in housekeeping by night and attends nursing school by day. Marcy walks into the house and goes straight to the kitchen. Aunt Earnestine's in there with Sidney cooking breakfast while Grandma and Grandpa are in the living room, still yelling at Uncle Ray about what happened early this morning.

"Hey, baby boy! Were you good for everybody last night while I was at work?" she asks as she's looking toward the living room and sees her parents talking to Ray, who doesn't seem too happy.

"What's going on in there?" she inquires.

"Girl, you won't believe what our crazy brother did last night! He had Trina Murphy half-naked in the hallway at 2:00 in the morning. Woke up everybody," she says in disgust. "Poor Sidney had to see it all. He bumped into her on his way to the bathroom. And crazy Ray told him he'd give him five dollars not to tell anybody."

"Trina Murphy from high school?" Marcy asks. "The girl with eleven toes!"

"Ooooooh, I wish Momma and Daddy would get him out of this house! He's in his twenties and acting like a teenager. I'm glad to be finishing nursing school so me and Sidney can get our own place. Working nights at the hospital and going to school in the daytime is tough enough without having to deal with this mess!"

Both Earnestine and Marcy are looking into the living room at their parents lecturing their baby brother.

"You know they're not kicking him out," says Earnestine.

She continues, "You know since daddy's getting older and had his heart attack, he needs Ray to help him out around the farm. Daddy can't do everything he used to do!"

"But is it worth putting up with Rays foolishness?" Asks Marcy.

Meanwhile, Ray is in the living room getting a stern talking to by his parents for what transpired just a few hours ago.

"Ray, you need to stop messing around with all these women," says Grandma.

"You should be ashamed of what you're doing son, and you're doing it right in front of your nephew," says Grandpa. "I didn't raise you like this. And your poor little nephew, Sidney, had to see a half-naked woman in the hallway at 2:00 in the morning." says grandma.

Uncle Ray just slumps down into the couch while he's being lectured.

"People in town are talking," says Grandpa in an angry voice. "Last month, I almost got into a fight with old man Johnson at the feed store. He was mad at me because you stood his daughter up on a date. The poor girl was sitting home crying to him all night. So when he sees me, he gives me a piece of his mind for something I didn't have nothing to do with."

Grandma and Grandpa have no clue where Ray's behavior comes from. However, Ray does. And while he's listening to them yell at him, his mind flashes back to 15 years earlier when Ray was nine years old.

****

It was a sunny day in Red Back, Louisiana. And little Ray is happy to be taking piano lessons. He and his mother are on the way to Louise Miller's house so Ray can have his first piano lesson. He's excited as he's been listening to people on the radio like Jerry Lee Lewis and Little Richard. He's listened to some of the great artists of the time and he can't wait to learn how to play the piano. His mother, Betty, is dropping him off for two hours and will pick him up later. Ray runs up the sidewalk leading to Miss Miller's house with excitement.

"Ray, baby, don't run, you're gonna trip," says Betty as she tries to calm Ray down. "Momma, hurry up!" he exclaims. "I can't wait to start. I gotta learn how to play like the guys on the radio!"

He's very excited as he knocks very loudly on the door at the small, modest house of Miss Miller. She answers the door with a warm and welcoming smile on her face.

"Why, hello, Ray!" She says as she looks at him and his mother, who's just getting to her doorstep.

"Hey, Miss Miller! Can you teach me how to play like Stevie Wonder or Little Richard?" Ray asks.

"Well, Ray, let's get started with the basic keys first and we'll see how that goes," says the young, single, librarian.

"Well, I've got to go finish up dinner. I'll be back at five to pick him up," says Betty, as she's looking at both Ray and Louise.

"Now Ray, don't give her any problems, ok young man!"

"I won't Mom!"

After making sure Ray is safe, Betty heads back to the farm to finish cooking dinner. In the meantime, Miss Miller welcomes young Ray into her home and takes him into the piano room.

"Ray, before we get started, how does some milk and cookies sound?" she asks Ray with excitement.

"Sounds good to me! And then can we get started?" Ray asks, eagerly anticipating his first piano lesson.

"Slow down Ray, we're gonna get started shortly," she says as Ray sits in front of the piano while she's still in the kitchen.

Miss Miller brings Ray a small plate with cookies and some milk.

"So, Ray, after you finish your cookies, we're going to start with the basic keys," she says as she starts rubbing his back.

He doesn't think anything of it as he's enjoying the warm baked chocolate chip cookies.

"Ray, can you keep a secret?" she asks hesitatingly.

"Umm, sure Miss Miller." he says. Miss Miller puts her hand on Ray's thigh and leans in unexpectedly and kisses Ray.

He's confused, but doesn't think anything of it and kisses her back.

"Well now, Ray, let's get started," she says, as though everything is fine.

Over the next few years, Ray continues to take lessons from Miss Miller. His parents have no idea what's going on between their son and his piano teacher.

****

"Why son, what are you thinking?" says Grandpa as Ray is brought back to the present day with his parents yelling at him after last night's events.

"Look, Mama, it wasn't my idea to move back here to the farm. I was doing good in the city. I had a job, an apartment and I was having fun. Y'all called me when Daddy had his heart attack and nobody else could help him on the farm. I dropped everything I had and came back here. And I been working hard getting up at five in the morning to feed cows and slop hogs. If I want to have some fun with nice young ladies, I should be able to do that!" says Ray sternly to his parents.

"Boy, you watch your tone!" yells grandpa.

"Daddy I'm sorry, but I got to have a life outside of the farm," says Ray. "OK, maybe it wasn't a good idea bringing that girl here this morning. But remember, I'm still young and I want to have fun." "Son, you can have fun, all the fun you want, but you need to be respectable and responsible. I don't want you to be like these no-good boys running around here with all these kids and not even married," says Grandma. "Ray, our family is better than that and we have a reputation to uphold as good, hardworking and respectable people," she continues.

2 CHAPTER
FRESH ROSES

After last night's excitement, Sidney and Grandpa are fishing on the farm as they do from time to time. This is the place where Grandpa usually gives young Sidney advice and wisdom about life that he can carry into adulthood. Since Sidney's dad is not in his life, Grandpa is making sure to give him all the advice he can from his many years of living. One thing for sure, grandpa has plenty of advice for Sidney, however, it's not always clear if Sidney's paying attention to these life lessons he's getting at such a young age.

"Make sure you bait that hook the right way son," says Grandpa.

"I did, Grandpa. I made sure to double-knot my fishing line like you always tell me."

"Good boy! Sidney, you know I'm proud of you?"

"Thanks! Grandpa, can I ask you a question? Who was that lady in the hallway last night?"

"That, Sid, was something that should've never happened. And you should have never seen it either. Your uncle Ray, is a good guy. He's smart and hard-working and I really love him, since he's my only son. But he doesn't always use his head. Sid, your uncle Ray does some dumb things. But you know what? I want you to learn from his foolishness. The way he treats women is not the way women are to be treated. One day you'll find you a nice girl. And later on, you're probably gonna marry her. Now, I want you to always take care of that woman and your family. Let her be the only girl in your life. You see son, a man isn't supposed to be running around with different women when he's married. One day you're gonna give a girl your heart. And, she's gonna give you hers. Now, when she does, you take good care of it. Treat her like she's a queen and make sure you provide for your family by doing a good honest day's work. You see how you take care of that goldfish in your room? You provide for it, don't ya?"

"Yes, Sir."

"You protect it, don't ya?"

"Yes, Sir," says Sidney as he's looking down at his fishing line.

"Well, that's how you treat that special girl when God puts her in your life. You provide for and protect her. You make her feel safe and secure. This family has had some issues with people not being able to commit to the people that love and take care of them. But I want you to be the link that breaks that chain of fooling around. Okay?" asks Grandpa.

"Umm, Okay, Grandpa," Sidney responds.
While sitting on the bank fishing with Sidney, Grandpa's mind goes back to a time when he and his wife, Betty, were young and newly-married.

****

It was 1954 and young Charlie Rivers was coming back to town from selling his crop at the buyer's mill. It was a good year for Charlie and his crop. He got more money from the buyers then he anticipated. He was due to come back in town on a Wednesday but he decided to come back on Tuesday to tell his wife Betty, about the good news of extra money. But before heading to the farm, he decides to stop and pick up some roses for his sweet wife who's been handling the farm and their first daughter, Marcy, for the last two days while he was gone. He stops at the Red Back Flower Shop, where Mrs. Connie O'Neal is more than happy to see him.

"Why hello Charlie, what brings you in?"

"Well, I wanna get a dozen of your best roses for my pretty little wife."

"Oh, really? What's the occasion?"

"We did pretty good with our crop this year and I wanna surprise her with that good news and I know the roses will make it extra special."

"Oh Charlie, you devil," says Mrs. O'Neal. "Well, let me get you some of the prettiest roses we have." She turns around and starts looking at her supply of roses. She bends over in a flirtatious way with her butt in the air to pick up a fresh bouquet from a crate. She's wearing a tight skirt in front of Charlie and asks, "Charlie, you like this?"

"Why yes, Mrs. O'Neal, I'm sure MY WIFE will love those," he says very sternly.

"Oh, Okay. Well, Charlie, here's a beautiful vase for your roses. Looks like you're gonna have a good night tonight," she says seductively.

"How much do I owe you?" Charlie asks, purposely ignoring Mrs. O'Neal's flirtation.

"That'll be $4.75."

"Here you go, Mrs. O'Neal, and you keep the change."

He turns and walks toward the door. Meantime, Mrs. O'Neal rushes from behind the counter to catch him at the door to jump in front of him.

"Charlie, you know Mr. O'Neal is out of town on business for the next two weeks and I need a man's touch around the house to do a few things. You think you can come by and help me out?"

"Well, what exactly do you need, Mrs. O'Neal?"

"Let's just say I have some plumbing issues."

"Well, Mrs. O'Neal, I have the perfect guy for that, old man Rainey over at the hardware store. He knows anything and everything about plumbing."

"What?" she asks, looking puzzled.

"Well, I've got to be going now, Mrs. O'Neal and I'll make sure to tell old man Rainey to come by and take care of that plumbing issue for you." Charlie says as he steps around her, pulls the door open and heads out of the flower shop and down the sidewalk to his truck. On the way to the truck, he passes two lady friends of him and his wife.

"Oh Charlie, Betty's gonna love those roses," says one of the women.

"I hope she does," says Charlie.

He keeps walking without breaking his confident stride to his truck. As the ladies keep walking, one says, after they pass Charlie, "Oh that is one good-looking man!"

"Oh, he is so dreamy," replies the other.

****

Charlie's on his way home and driving down the dirt road leading to his farmhouse. He's excited to see Betty and their baby, Marcy. His old Chevy truck kicks up dust from behind as it gets closer to the farmhouse. He and Betty worked hard and saved all they could to buy it. He's ready to surprise her with an early arrival and the roses he picked up. After parking on the driveway made of dead grass and dirt, he notices a car parked behind the house. Betty's friends from the baking club usually park there because of the shade of a large peach tree. Their bedroom window is open as well with the white crisp curtains blowing in breeze. Charlie walks up to the front porch and he notices both the screen and front doors are closed. Usually they keep the front door open to get a refreshing breeze flowing through the house. Walking through the front door quietly to surprise his wife, he notices baby Marcy is asleep in her bassinette in the living room. Betty is probably in the kitchen, so Charlie heads that way with flowers in hand. He passes their bedroom, which has music coming out of it from an old radio. Charlie pushes the door open with anticipation of seeing Betty and he's frozen by what he sees. Betty's in bed with another man. She and the man are both startled at his presence.

"Charlie!" Betty screams.

"Now, now look here, Mister, I don't want no trouble," the man says as his voice trembles with fright.

Charlie is his usual calm, cool and collected self. He turns to the left and walks to his large oak dresser. Both Betty and her co-adulterer are frantically hurrying to get dressed. The man scrambles to put on his pants and shirt while neglecting to pull up his suspenders. He throws his shoes out the window as he's trying to climb out.

"Charlie, I'm sorry!" screams Betty.

Charlie pulls out a double barrel shotgun from the dresser drawer.

"No Charlie, No Charlie!" Betty screams from the bed as Charlie runs out the room toward the front door.

The man finally made it to his car. As he's speeding past the side of the house to get to the driveway, cool, calm and collected Charlie Rivers pumps one shot into the back driver side door of the car with his precise aim.

The man screams with fright. Charlie pulls the trigger a second time and this time he shoots out the back window. He can see the man's head ducking and still screaming as the glass shatters. The car is out of his sight now and all that's left is a trail of dust.

"Grandpa, I got one! Grandpa, I got one!" a voice screams out loud. Sidney has just brought his Grandpa back to present day, where the two of them are fishing and Sidney's hooked a nice big catfish on the end of his line.
"Well, go easy on it, Sidney, and don't let him get loose from ya," Grandpa yells as he helps Sidney bring in this whopper of a fish.

Later that day, there's a graduation party for Sidney's mom, Marcy. She's finally finished nursing school. Everyone is down at the farm for the party and having a good time. There's a disc jockey playing some old rhythm and blues and everyone's having fun. Grandpa is playing dominoes with some of his friends. Uncle Ray is dancing with two women. Aunt Earnestine and Marcy, who's proudly wearing her graduation cap, are playing cards with two longtime friends, while Grandma and some other ladies are preparing food.

"So Marcy, how does it feel to be through with school?" one of the friends asks.

"Girl, it feels so good! I been cleaning toilets and mopping at night for the last three years while going to school. I told 'em yesterday I've cleaned my last toilet while working in housekeeping and it's time for me to start making real money as a nurse," Marcy says with pride.

 "I know that's right! I'm so proud of my big sister," says Earnestine.

"Thanks sis! I couldn't have did it without your help by watching and taking care of Sidney for me. I'm supposed to meet with the head nurse on Monday to see where they plan to start me out in the hospital."

"Sid! Sid!" Grandpa yells. "Hey, go light this cigar for me on the stove!"

Sidney, excited, agrees to go light the cigar for Grandpa on the family's gas stove in the kitchen. For whatever reason, Grandpa doesn't carry a lighter. Sidney is always happy to do this because it allows him to take a few puffs off the cigar before he brings it back to his grandfather. He taught himself how to make smoke come out of his mouth and nose while pretending he's a dragon. Sidney's been doing this since the age of five. You would think his Grandpa would notice the cigar butt is semi-wet when he puts the cigarette in his mouth, but he never says anything about it.

Meantime while the ladies are playing spades, the two women at the party with Uncle Ray get into an argument over who owes whom for gas money on their way back home. They're from out of town and Ray met them and a host of other women when he moved away from the farm for a little while. Now, these ladies are very attractive, with perfect hourglass shapes. A lot of the men, both young and old, including Grandpa's friends, cautiously sneak a peek at the women to avoid getting caught by their wives. Strangely, these ladies made the long drive down to see Ray and get some free barbecue. As usual, there's drama with Ray and his girlfriends. This time, one has had too much to drink and she's getting loud and obnoxious in front of all the guests. Ray gets in the middle, trying to break it up.

Grandma Betty is sitting with some other women her age in lawn chairs. She's clearly annoyed by the behavior of Ray's guest.

"Ray, if you don't get those crazy fools away from this house!" Grandma Betty yells, shaking her head.

"I just don't know where he gets it from."

"Look at them skanks," says Gertrude, her longtime friend. "They probably got that new disease called the dirties."

"Gert, I think you mean the herpes," says Mrs. Tippins.

"Well, whatever. They look like they got something."

****

It's Monday morning at the Red Back Community Hospital. Marcy's anxiously waiting in the hallway by human resources to meet with Doris, the head nurse of the hospital. She's finishing up with another nurse and walking her to the door. As she says goodbye to the other lady, she notices Marcy sitting in the hallway. "Hey, Marcy! How are you doing? Congratulations on finishing nursing school! I know how hard you worked and you definitely earned it!"

"Thanks, Doris."

"Well, come on in and have a seat."

"Okay!" says Marcy with excitement as she walks behind Nurse Doris into the office.

Marcy is really excited to find out where and what department she'll be working in.

"Well, Marcy, I've got good news and I've got not so good news. What do you want to hear first?"

"Umm," Marcy says looking puzzled.

"Okay, here's the good news. We want to offer you a nursing position. The not so good news is it's a nursing position in New Orleans."

"New Orleans? That's an hour and a half away from here."

"I know it is. But with the big new hospital being built there, the company needs a lot of nurses to fill positions to make it successful. Those are the only positions we have available, and if you decide to take it, the hospital will pay your moving expenses."

This was tough news for Marcy. She's been in Red Back her entire life. She'd planned on staying in town and working as a nurse while being close to her family after she graduated from nursing school.

****

Well after much thought and prayer, Marcy agreed to take the position in New Orleans. And it's now moving day.
Marcy and her son Sidney found a house in New Orleans. The whole family came up to help them move in. It's a nice, middle class neighborhood. While helping uncle Ray and Grandpa Charlie unload the moving truck, Sidney's attention turns toward two girls sitting in the driveway across the street. One of them has

his attention more than the other. Uncle Ray notices Sidney checking out the girls.

"Hey man! So, what's up?" Ray asks Sidney.

"What's up with what?" a puzzled Sidney responds.

"Don't try to play me like a fool. I see you checking out them girls over there. Go introduce yourself."

Sidney's shaking his head to disagree.

"Look here. See, I need to make sure we're leaving my big sister here with a man and not some little scared punk. Just go over there, introduce yourself and let them know you're new to the neighborhood and you want them to show you around sometime."

Looking nervous, Sidney says, "I'ma go later on."

Ray unexpectedly pushes Sidney out of the moving trailer.

"Boy, get over there!"

The girls across the street start giggling. There's no turning back now. He nervously starts walking toward them. When he gets about 10 feet away, he feels a tap on the shoulder. He turns and looks at a husky and beefy-looking girl. She looks to be the oldest of the other two girls. She's looking mean and downward at Sidney.

"Can I help you?" she asks. "Is there something you need?"

Luckily, though Sidney is unaware, one of the two girls in the driveway has walked up behind him as he's looking at the husky girl with fear. She jumps in to save him.

"Hi, I'm Karen," she says. "This is my sister, Sheila." She points to the other girl still sitting in the driveway.

"And that's my sister Debra, who you've already met."

"Hey, I'm Sidney. We're moving in across the street."

"So what grade are you in?" Karen asks.

"I'm in the seventh grade!" Sidney's still somewhat nervous with the pressure of the girls good looks and the mean glare of the protective big sister.

"I'm in seventh grade, too. Looks like you'll probably be going to my school."

"Alright. Well, nice meeting you. I've got to help finish moving." And Sidney rushes off.

"Nice meeting you, Sidney!" Karen yells.

After hearing her sweet voice yell his name, he's feeling fortunate. Sidney stops in his tracks and turns around with an undeniable blush and tells her, "See you later."

Still looking suspiciously at Sidney, Debra, the oldest sister, had to somewhat sour the moment with, "Yeah ... *we'll* see you later."

Uncle Ray is in the back of the trailer checking out everything across the street. He's grinning and proud of Sidney. As he's walking back to the truck, his face has a look of relief on it as though he's completed a big challenge or task. He looks at uncle Ray who gives him a grin of acceptance and a thumbs up.

3 CHAPTER
LOVE BIRDS

Sidney and Karen become childhood sweethearts. They start walking to school together in the early years of junior high. They often eat lunch together and are inseparable. Sidney frequently walks Karen to her classes and carries her books. Karen runs track and wins several state championships for their high school varsity track team. Sometimes Sidney waits until Karen's track practice is over and walks her home.

Sidney is a handsome-looking guy and other girls would often give him the flirting eye. But one girl has his heart throughout his teenage years.

Sidney's mom, Marcy, really likes Karen a lot. Karen's mother is a single parent as well and she gets along good with Sidney's mom. In high school, Karen and Sidney were voted the cutest couple and had one of the best looking prom pics as Karen was voted prom queen.

After high school, the young couple planned to attend the same college, but Karen got a track scholarship to a school in Northern Louisiana while Sidney got an academic scholarship to a college nearby in New Orleans. It was rough on the two of them, since they'd been together since junior high school. Things were a little rocky at first, but their relationship survived the separation caused by college. After they both graduated, Karen moved back to New Orleans. Not long after that, Sidney proposed to her. As expected, she said 'yes."

Nine years after graduating college, Sidney and Karen have a nice upper middle class house in New Orleans. The neighborhood is filled with lawns that are maintained with straight edges and beautiful flowers. Good landscaping is a requirement of their homeowners' association. Their driveway has a nice black Range Rover parked in it. In the garage, there's a BMW station wagon which they call the "mom mobile." Karen uses it to take their seven-year-old daughter, Ally, and her friends to school and to various activities, such as dance and soccer practice. Inside their lovely two-story house, there are pictures on the wall of Karen and Sidney with their diplomas, their wedding photos and one of them holding their daughter in the hospital right after she was born. Karen is a stay-at-home mom and wife while Sidney runs an accounting firm with his business partner, Howard, whom he met in college.

On this morning, Karen's cooking breakfast while Sidney's upstairs getting ready to go to the office. She's watching the morning news on a small flat screen in the kitchen. Their daughter, Ally, is in the living room watching cartoons. Sidney's ready to start the day as he's coming downstairs with his suit and tie on.

Ally runs to give her dad a hug as he comes downstairs.

"Morning, Daddy!" she says with excitement.

"Morning, Baby Girl!!! You excited about school today?"

"Yep! And I'm ready for my spelling test, too."

"What's the plan?" Sidney asks since he wants to make sure his daughter starts out planning for life at an early age.

"Get a scholarship. Go to college and start a business like you," says Ally.

"That's my girl! I'm so proud of you," Sidney says as he picks her up and kisses her.

He puts her down and walks into the kitchen to greet Karen. She's enticed by something on the news while wearing her apron and holding a spatula.

Sidney walks up behind her, grabs her waist and whispers in her ear, "Morning, beautiful!"

"Can you believe this? Two 12-year-old boys robbed an 84-year-old lady at the mall yesterday and went shopping with her credit cards." Turning from the TV, she looks at Sidney and says, "Thanks for last night."

"No. Thank you!" he says as he leans in to grab a quick kiss on her lips.

"Yeah…I'm not surprised," he replies. "These kids today are going crazy. They're walking around with their jeans sagging and underwear showing. A lot of them don't have a good male figure to teach 'em right from wrong. So instead they're looking up to the streets for role models."

"That's why it's important that we keep praying for our future son-in-law … wherever he is now," Karen says as she sets the breakfast plates on the table in the kitchen. "We're going to keep praying that his parents are making him into a Godly man so that by the time he meets our little princess, he'll be a good, hard-working Christian man like you," she says while looking in the living room at Ally as she's watching TV. "Ally, come eat, baby!"

"Hey, I'm going to ride to the office with Howard today. We've got to go meet with two clients this morning. I might have you pick me up later at the office or have him drop me off back here."

"No problem," Karen says, nodding her head. "I just want you to be careful around Howard and all those crazy women he messes with. I remember the last one that came down to office and y'all had to call security on her."

"Look, Howard's a single guy doing the single guy thing. Not everybody is as lucky as me to have such a wonderful wife. He knows as my business partner that I'm all about business and I don't have time to get caught up with his foolishness and crazy women. But in all seriousness, he and I built this business from the ground up and the dude knows his stuff when it comes to accounting. And he knows that I'm a happily married man to one of the greatest women in the world and nothing is going to mess this up."

"Okay, just watch yourself, honey." Karen warns.

There's a honk from a car outside.

"There he is. I'll see you guys this evening." Sidney kisses Karen and tells Ally to come hug him before he leaves. "Have fun at school, baby girl," he tells her as he's walking out the front door.

Sidney comes out the front door and is surprised to see a black, four-door Mercedes since Howard owns a Corvette.

As he gets in, he asks Howard, "How did you go from driving a two-door, bachelor Corvette to this?"

"It's not mine," says Howard. "I got another stalker. This belongs to one of my neighbors. He let me use it while he's out of town. This crazy psycho's been following me for the last two days. So I thought I'd change it up on her. I've got dark windows … he's got dark windows, so you can't see inside. Plus, my neighbor is an old guy who's having a midlife crisis, so he loves driving my 'Vette. It makes him feel younger."

"Bro, you better stop messing with these crazy women. Didn't you learn your lesson from a couple of weeks ago?"

"You had to bring that up, didn't you? I'm trying to get that out of my mind man!"

"Man how could you forget that? That was too funny!" Sidney says laughing as he reminisces about what happened a few weeks earlier.

A few weeks back, around four in the afternoon, Howard got a call from a lady who said she was interested in having him do some accounting for her large company. The lady said she'd like to meet around 5:30 and get signed up with the company to fix her accounting problems. She made it seem as though it was very urgent that they meet that evening. So Howard decides to go meet the lady at her office. Once he arrived at what seemed to be an industrial warehouse area, he opens the door of the office number she gave him. Suddenly, Howard was blinded with pepper spray. He couldn't see anything. He heard voices that seemed to come from several people. He figured they were women by the smell of perfume and body spray. The voices sounded familiar even though the women tried to disguise themselves by talking with fake deep voices as though they were men. The ladies held him down, blind folded and tied his hands behind his back. All while Howard was yelling and screaming, "My eyes! My eyes!"

"Shut up!" One of the women said as she forgot to disguise her voice.

"I mean, shut up." she says again but this time she remembered to make her voice deep like a man.

"We'll show you....since you want to play with people's hearts," another lady says.

"Whoever this is, I'm sorry! I'm sorry!"

"Sure you are!"

"Pull the van around!" said one of the women as deep as she could but it was obvious she was struggling to sound like a man.

"Come on guys! Who is this? Heather? Michelle? Audrey? Who is this?"

The groups of people/kidnappers hurry up and rush him outside to a van. Howards screaming and yelling the entire way but he can't overcome the group as they shove him into the back of a van. No one is around to hear his distress calls. After what seemed like a very long ride for Howard, the van came to a stop.

"Take his clothes off!"

"What?" Howard yells.

"The group immediately jumps on him and starts taking off his shoes, socks, belt etc...

After fighting and struggling, Howard is down to his boxer shorts.

"Take those off too!" yells one women who came out of character, not disguising her voice.

"Um guys...would that be too mean?" One voice says.

"Yeah guys that would be too mean!" yells Howard.

"Whoever this is, I'm sorry! Tina, Tonya...Diane!"

"You are so pathetic!" one woman yells.

"Ok just hold him still."

"Hey! Hey! What is that! What are you doing?"

Howard feels something on his body and he doesn't know what it is. It kind of tickles and they've used it on his back, stomach shoulders and thighs. He tries to fight but can't since they all sat on top of him to hold him down.

The door of the van slides open.

"This is where you get off buddy!" shouts one of the voices.

Howard feels someone pushing him out while he's blindfolded with his hands still tied behind his back and lands on his side in what feels like grass.

Next he hears the van taking off as the driver is flooring it to get away as quickly as possible.

Howards was in the grass and struggling to get his hands free but can't.

He's managed to slide the blind fold off by rubbing his face on the ground and got to his feet to see what was around him.

He's in a rough part of town. There's run down, vacant houses and vacant lots all around him. A couple of guys who look to be homeless walk up to him and ask, "Hey man! Are you ok?"

"Help me guys! Help me! Untie my hands, please!"

"Sir, you don't have any clothes on. I aint touching you!" one man says as he's walking off.

Eventually Howard got free and made it to a phone after being rejected by several people in the neighborhood. He looked like a deranged drug addict as he was knocking on doors begging for help. After he promised to pay an elderly man to use his phone, he was able to call Sidney to come and pick him up and bring some cash to pay the guy for using his phone. That ticklish feeling Howard had when he was tied up? Lipstick! The women had written all kinds of words on his body in red lipstick. Words such as cheater, liar, two timer and other words that a scorned woman would use.

"Hey can you not bring that up? I'm trying to move on!"

Howard says as he's driving and Sidney is reminiscing and laughing about the kidnapping.

"Man that's not funny! I could have been killed!"

"Yeah that lipstick could have killed you!" Sidney jokes.

"I'm glad you find it funny. I ain't worried about it. Every chick wants a little Howard in their life."

"You need to come to church with us. There's some really good women there with their heads on straight," Sidney advises.

"Let me stop you there, partner! I've tried the church women thing. They want to go straight to the wedding. Dang! Can we date first?"

"All right, bro. Keep playing, I don't know how many more busted car windows and bomb threats we can take at the office. Let's get to these meetings and swing by the office to see how the renovation is going afterwards," Sidney says.

Howard is shaking his head with frustration and adds, "This renovation is really becoming a pain in the butt. I don't know how much more of this I can take. They're already two weeks behind and over budget. Luis called me last night about one of his guys getting into it with Melvin's guys. Who would have ever thought we'd be keeping Luis' painters from getting into it with Melvin's electrical guy. It's like a gang fight: the painters versus the electricians."

"Melvin should look out for Luis," Sidney mentions. "I heard Luis is no punk. I was talking to one of his guys and he told me Luis was a golden glove boxer back in the day."

Sidney and Howard go and meet with two of their most important clients, which they do regularly to make sure the clients are happy. They've worked hard to get their accounting firm off the ground and now with an influx of new clients the past few years, their business has skyrocketed. The clients love them because they're young, aggressive and smart. They're snappy dressers who make a point of looking good on every client visit. Their suits, shirts and ties are stylish, giving them a look of success, and the right cologne gives them the smell of money.

Sidney met Howard while in college and the two of them hit it off immediately. Howard is a character, who always finds a way to make people laugh in meetings. Many of the clients like his witty personality combined with Sidney's keen business sense.

On the way to the meeting, they see some teenage kids walking down the street with their pants sagging.

"I don't get this sagging look," Sidney says in disgust. "I can't wrap my head around it. Why would you want to walk around with people looking at your underwear? How are people supposed to take you seriously?"

"Well, I know a lot of them don't have a good home and have no dad," Howard says.

"That's no excuse. I didn't grow up with a dad and you see how I turned out."

While at a stoplight and in the passenger seat, Sidney manages to make eye contact with a teenager who's waiting at a bus stop. The two of them stare at each other. Sidney is looking at the kid with his school uniform which consists of khakis and a polo shirt. He's sagging in his khakis even though he has on a belt. It's as though they are having a stare down competition. Out of nowhere, the kid flips him off when the light turns green as Howard speeds off.

CHAPTER 4
THE RIGHT PATH

It's Sunday morning. Sidney and his family are at church. Pastor T.D. Jakes is the guest pastor today and he's bringing an encouraging word. After church, as Sidney and his family are walking to their Range Rover, Deacon Miller approaches them in the parking lot. He walks up to Sidney after he's held the door open for Karen and Ally to get in on the passenger side.

"Hey, Sidney I've been trying to catch up with you. You're a busy man."

"Well Deacon, we've been busy at the office and I'm trying to juggle time with my family as well. What's up?"

"Sidney, I need you to do me a favor. You know we've started a mentoring program here at the church to reach the community. I've got a kid that I know you'd make a good mentor to. He's got a single mom taking care of him, but he needs a strong male mentor like you. He's a good kid, but he lives in a bad neighborhood. So, what you think, Sidney? Can I put you down as a mentor?"

Sidney doesn't sound too sure as he tells Deacon Miller, "Well Deacon, I'm pretty busy right now at the office and I have a major remodel going on there as well. I really have to think about it to make sure I can fit it in my schedule."

"Let me know your decision as soon as possible. Promise me you'll give it some serious thought, Sidney?"

"Deacon, you have my word. I will think about it and let you know."

Sidney hops in the Range Rover with Karen and Ally. They're going to his mother, Marcy's house after church for Sunday dinner.

Karen saw Sidney and Deacon Miller talking outside the car but she couldn't hear their conversation.

"I am starving. I can't wait to taste some of mom's smoked turkey!" Sidney says.

Sounding curious, Karen asks, "And what was that all about?"

"It was about nothing. He was asking me about joining a mentoring program to some kid. I told him I've got a lot going on with the company right now, though."

"Are you kidding me? You have the chance to mentor some kid, impact his life and you're not even going to give it some serious thought? Sidney, just think about those boys who robbed that lady at the mall. I bet they didn't have any mentors or strong men like you in their lives. If they did, I'm sure they would have never robbed her."

"Geez, has the deacon talked to you about this already?"

"No Sidney, he hasn't! But doesn't it make sense? Look, you don't have a son right now and maybe this'll be some training for you and it'll be good for you to help out some kid."

"Babe, look! I'm really tied down with the company right now. We're bringing on four new clients this month plus this crazy renovation is taking a toll on me. And I'm trying to spend as much time with you and Ally as possible."

"I know you're busy. But I don't think it'll hurt you to spend a few hours a month with a kid as a mentor. I think you should do it! Sounds like it'll be fun."

Later on Sunday evening, Sidney tries to wind down. It's been a long day for him and his family. An early Sunday breakfast, church and dinner at his mother's house, not to mention a one-hour call from Howard about an important conference call with a very big client tomorrow. He's glad to finally hit the sack and get some rest. While Sidney's sleeping, he starts having a crazy dream. In his dream he's at home with Karen in the kitchen. Karen is telling Sidney that a boy from Ally's school is picking her up to go to a school dance. He asks if she knows the boy's parents. She doesn't. She says that from everything Ally has told her, he's one of the nicest boys in her school.

Sidney hears some loud music coming from outside. Then the doorbell rings. Ally comes running downstairs with excitement. "Stewart is here! See you guys later," she says as she's getting her purse. Sidney tells her to hold on.

Sidney answers the door and it's a thuggish-looking kid with loud music playing from his car parked in front of the house. He's got on a white tank top, heavy-starched sagging jeans that are exposing his boxer shorts. He's got two gold teeth and his baseball cap is turned to the side on his head. "Hey, Where's ya daughter at?" the kid asks with a total lack of respect.

Suddenly Sidney wakes up from his nightmare in a cold sweat.

The next day while on his way to the office, he calls Deacon Miller and commits to joining the mentor program. If he can keep one kid from becoming like the kid in his dream from last night, well that's more than enough help. Deacon Miller gives Sidney the contact information of the family he's going to be mentoring. He gives Sidney some background information as well. His name is Josh and his mom is Denise. She's a single mom who works in the kitchen at a hotel in downtown New Orleans. Josh is a good kid with decent grades, but at any moment, he could go down the wrong path because of the neighborhood and the absence of his mother, who works long hours to pay the bills.

A few days later, Sidney heads out to meet Josh and his mother for the first time. As he's driving to their apartment, he sees people standing around and hanging out on the corner. There's a big domino game going on under a shade tree with a large group of people gathered around it. Driving through the low-income neighborhood, the Range Rover sticks out like a sore thumb. People turn and stare at it. Sidney pulls up to the apartment building where Josh lives with his mother Denise. He told them he'd be there at 4 p.m. As he gets out, he takes a look around the parking lot and checks his surroundings as a measure of caution, since this is not the best neighborhood in the world.

In front of his parking space he sees an elderly lady sitting on her patio which has no fence or gate surrounding it.

"You must be Sidney," she says.

"Yes ma'am. I am. Are you Denise?"

"Oh no! I'm too old to be Denise. I'm Ms. Ella. Denise and Josh live up stairs above my apartment. They're running late because of Denise's car, but she's on her way, though. Have a seat."

Sidney looks down and the seat is an upside-down plastic milk crate with a rocking chair cushion on top. He wants to tell her, "No that's alright, I'll stand," but he doesn't want to hurt the feelings of an elderly lady he just met. With his 6-foot-4-inch frame, he squats down and sits on the crate.

"They didn't tell us you would be so good looking, Sidney!"

"Well thank you ma'am," he says. "Well you can just call me Ms. Ella. That ma'am stuff makes me feel old. Let me tell you, I think it's great that Josh is going to have a mentor to look up to. We need more men like you stepping in to guide these kids in single mom households. Josh is a good kid. Denise tries to do everything she can for him. His dad's nowhere to be found. But she holds it down by herself pretty good.

Every now and then he'll try to do something crazy, like most boys do at his age. I step in when she needs some help. But it's something about a man's presence to guide him. That's why I talked to Deacon Miller about enrolling Josh into the mentoring program, and he highly recommended you. I've known Denise all her life. Her mother and I were best friends from our teenage years and I raised Denise from a baby since her mother committed..."

"Hey, Ms. Ella!" several voices yell out of nowhere and interrupts her story. It's some neighborhood kids passing by in the parking lot on their bikes, going fast, jumping over speed bumps like daredevils.

"Hey, you boys, be careful in this parking lot and watch out for cars!"

As Sidney and Ms. Ella are talking, an older model sedan pulls up next to his parked car with a lady and a teenage boy in the passenger seat. They get out. The kid is admiring the Range Rover as he's walking past it. He's holding some plastic sacks along with a backpack slung over one shoulder. They start walking toward Sidney and Ms. Ella. The teenager looks really familiar to Sidney for some reason. He's got on a school uniform with his shirt tucked in and his pants pulled up like he's working for Target or Best Buy. The lady with him looks to be in her late twenties or early thirties. She's a very beautiful-looking lady with her hair pinned up to catch air and keep her neck cool. By the looks of things, she's had a long day. It's obvious she works in some kind of restaurant or kitchen, as she's wearing a uniform that consists of a white chef's shirt along with black-and-white-checkered pants with black sneakers. She hurries over to the patio from the car as she's clutching her purse, ignoring the shoulder straps as though she's late for some important meeting.

"Denise and Josh, this is Sidney from the mentoring program," shouts Ms. Ella.

"I'm Denise and this is Josh. Sorry about being late. My car wouldn't start and I had to get a jump start. I think the battery is going out. I had to wait on security at work to give me a boost, so that meant picking him up late from school. He rides the bus in the morning and I pick him up after school to make sure he gets home safe. Then I had to stop by the store to get some stuff for dinner."

She's rambling until Sidney jumps in and tells her, "Hey, it's alright!"

Denise has a look of relief on her face and appreciates his forgiveness. She looks as though she's able to get her taxes in on time at the last minute.

"I'm Sidney, and it's nice to meet you. I was just talking to Ms. Ella here and she was telling me about you guys."

"I hope it was all good. I know how Ms. Ella will tell you all of people's business," Denise says with a laugh.

Sidney then turns to Josh. In order to encourage him and break the ice, he says, "Hey what's up big man, how you doing?"

"I'm good. So, mom told me you're my dad!" says the kid boldly with 100 percent seriousness on his face.

There's an awkward moment of silence between all four of them.

"Ha, gotcha!" the kid says of his joke.

Sidney takes a deep breath of relief.

"Will you stop playing with people like that?" Denise says with authority. "This boy is a jokester. It almost got him in detention last week in school," she says shaking her head while looking at her son with a laugh on his face.

"Oh, I see you're, Mr. Funny Man!" says Sidney sarcastically.

"Hey, is that your Range Rover?" Josh asks.

"Yeah, it's mine!"

"Can I drive it?"

"Sure, man! Here's the key!

Josh's face has a look of surprise, like a kid on Christmas morning as he reaches for the keys.

As he sticks his hands out with excitement to get them, Sidney pulls them back and says, "Just kidding! I can be funny too!"

Denise and Ms. Ella erupt with laughter, while Josh has a look of disbelief on his face.

"Well, let's go upstairs so he can put this stuff up! Denise says.

Denise and Josh head upstairs as they're followed by Sidney. Ms. Ella sits back down on her padded milk crate so she can be the unofficial neighborhood look out.

As Sidney enters, he notices it's a modest apartment with very little on the walls except a few family photos all of Josh and Denise. The size of the entire two-bedroom apartment is almost the size of his theater room at home. Though it's not very big, it's clean and tidy. There's a striking smell of baked goods in the air.

"Excuse the mess. I was experimenting with some new cookie recipes and didn't get to put up everything."

She was referring to a stack of pans that seemed to be clean, but not put away. Sidney hadn't even noticed. The pans were stacked so neatly that they didn't look out of order to him.

"So you do a lot of cooking at home, too?" asks Sidney as he's scoping out the apartment. Josh has disappeared to one of the back bedrooms.

"Oh, yeah!" she says enthusiastically. "This is where I can really throw down. I specialize in pastries. I've been going to cooking school at night for the last two years to become a pastry chef. I'll be graduating next month.

I'm limited in what I can make at work, since I have to listen to the company. At home, I can create all kinds of desserts and sell a few to family and friends," she says, confident in her skills. Then she elaborates, "Well, mostly friends since we really don't have any family around."

"You guys aren't from here?" asks Sidney.

"We're from here but we just don't have any family," Denise explains. "My mother committed suicide when I was baby and Ms. Ella was her best friend. So she raised me by herself since she never had any kids. I wanted Ms. Ella to move in with us and I'd take care of her since she raised me. But she told me she's still got a lot of life in her and she wants her independence. So that's why she stays in the apartment downstairs and I'm upstairs where I can keep an eye on her and make sure that she's okay."

"I'm sorry about your mother. What about your dad?" Sidney inquires.

"Well aren't we a little nosy!" she answers with a serious look on her face.

"Oh I'm sorry," Sidney says with a look that says, "I just screwed up."

"I'm just messing with you,"

"I don't know my dad," she volunteers. "All I know is that he has a tattoo just like this on his right arm."

Denise holds up her right arm for Sidney to study. On her inner wrist is a small tattoo of the words "love easy and live fast" in cursive letters with two upside down hearts.

"Oh, wow!" says Sidney as he's noticing Denise's soft and flawless skin on her face.

She doesn't seem like a lady who should be stuck in this little apartment as a single mom having to work hard to make ends meet. She seems as though she deserves the life of his wife Karen, which consists of staying at home and only having to take care of the house and kids. But that wasn't her experience. She's a hardworking, beautiful, single mom who's had some tough times in life. But she's handled it with optimism as she tries to better herself.

"So you're not like one of those crazy pervert guys on the news messing around with little boys are you?" she says with a look of seriousness on her face.

"No!" says Sidney. "I'm a concerned parent as well. I'm always making sure my daughter is with safe people when she's not in my sight. So there's no funny business here," Sidney adds to assure Denise to let her know he's just hanging out with her son to be a mentor.

"Good, because I'm an ex-Marine and I still have my combat skills!"

"Here is my business card with all of my numbers." He hands her the crisp white card with a scent of cologne on it.

"All right. That little knucklehead in there is my knucklehead and I'll kill anybody that ever tried to hurt or harm him."

"I'd do the same and worse if it was involving my daughter," Sidney responds.

Denise looks at Sidney with a look of acceptance as to say, "I'm gonna trust you, but I will be keeping an eye on you at the same time."

Josh has now come from the back of the apartment having changed his clothes. He's traded in his neatly-pressed polo shirt and khakis for oversized shorts and an oversized shirt. His shorts have slight sag to them.

"Boy, if you don't pull those shorts up." Denise says like a mother who's about to do a windup pitch that will result in a slap instead of a fast ball.

"But, Mom!" Josh replies quickly.

"Hey, man, if you're going to roll with me, you're going to have to do better than that. I don't hang around with sloppy-looking people," Sidney says.

With a look of surrender, Josh raises his t-shirt up and pulls up the shorts and pulls the drawstring tightly so they can fit correctly around his waist.

"So where are you guys going to hang out?" Denise asks.

"We're going to go to the golf range and hit a few golf balls."

"Well have fun and don't you give him any problems, you understand me, Josh?"

Sidney and Josh head out. Denise walks them to the door. She keeps the door slightly cracked to peep out and look at Sidney from behind admiring his tall, athletic frame. As she's standing and spying, she puts Sidney's business card to her nose and she's enticed by the smell of cologne the card holds. Though it's a business card, it smells like a sample card given out in the men's cologne department at a fine upscale department store like Macy's or Nordstrom's. It's a smell of success and power and she likes it.

****

"Ally, get the ball! Get the ball!" Karen is on the other side of town at soccer practice for Ally while Sidney is meeting Josh for the first time.

"Karen, it's just a practice scrimmage!" exclaims Donna, whose daughter also plays on Ally's soccer team. She's a neighbor who lives a few houses down from Sidney and Karen.

"I know, but have you seen the team they're playing this Saturday? Those little girls are huge," she says while keeping her eyes and attention focused on Ally out on the field.

"Well, anyway, I told Thomas I really want him to keep his distance around this new temp they hired at the office. I brought him lunch and she's prancing around in this tight mini skirt, just being as friendly as she can be with her little skirt and cute, short, blond haircut."

"Donna, get over it! Thomas isn't going to mess around on you. He sends you flowers at home and he cooks for you when he comes home!" And even if he did, you'd know about it since I showed you how to track his cell phone calls . And he'll never be out of your sight with the GPS app I put on your phone." Karen says with assurance.

"Now, who you need to look out for is that neighbor across the street, Sheila."

Sheila is the new neighbor who has women in the neighborhood on edge because of her stunning good looks and outgoing personality. She moved into the neighborhood six months ago with her husband, who's an international banker. He travels around the world for long periods of time leaving her home alone on a regular basis. She's usually driving around the neighborhood in her red convertible Mercedes and large sunglasses, which give her that movie star look as though she has no cares in the world.

"Yeah, she always needs someone's husband to help her out with moving things or something around the house," says Donna. "She asked me if Thomas could come over and kill a big spider she saw in her kitchen. I told him he could go but he'd better be back in 10 minutes or I was coming over there in my rollers and house coat if I needed to."

"And you let him go?" Karen asks with a look of surprise. "I would've asked her, 'Does my husband look like an exterminator to you? Google one!'" says Karen.

"I took care of that already," Karen adds. "Now Donna, I don't need you going back and telling this to anyone?" Karen says in a demanding voice. "But the other night, while Sidney was in the shower, she comes and knocks on the door. It was around 7:30. I went to answer and she's there looking all innocent and she says, 'I hate to bother you, but I was wondering if your husband could come over and change a light bulb that's too high for me to reach.' I almost starting cursing and probably would have if Ally wasn't nearby in the study doing her homework!"

"Oh, my God!" Donna says in disbelief.

Karen continues with her story. "Well, anyway, I stepped outside and closed the door. I told her, 'I don't know you and I'm sure you're a nice lady, but it's not appropriate for my husband to be working at your house.' I also told her to never, ever, ever ask my husband to do anything for her if I'm not around. 'That means don't even ask him for a tissue if your nose is bleeding.'"

"Oh wow, a tissue, Karen?" asks Donna.

"Not even a tissue!" Karen says with a look of dire seriousness on her face. "I said, 'If I ever catch you talking to my husband while I'm not around, all hell will break loose and you will feel a wrath of pain you've never known existed. Try me!'"

"You have to be straightforward when you're protecting what's yours."

"You remember what happened to Jeff and Maria when he started cheating on her? I saw that one coming a mile away, when Jeff was suddenly working late with that pretty little secretary of his. I told Maria something wasn't right when he started coming home smelling like Victoria Secret body lotion that she couldn't wear because of her allergies. He started taking phone calls late at night, saying it was business. So one night, she and I paid a visit to his office, to bring him dinner, when he was supposedly working late and what did we find? Jeff and the secretary in the conference room … discussing some hard core business. So seeing stuff like that has me on the defensive to protect my most important asset, my husband."

****

Sidney and Josh have just finished hitting a few golf balls at the driving range. Sidney taught Josh how to hit a golf ball a long distance. To his surprise, Josh learned pretty quickly how to swing. Josh was hitting the ball pretty far for a beginner. They stopped and got something to eat before Sidney dropped Josh off. They had a great time talking about guy stuff such as sports, cars and girls. It was something that Josh really needed since he's never had a positive male in his life to talk with and hang out together. Afterward, they headed back to Josh's apartment where Denise was waiting. On the way back Sidney uses this time to give Josh some wisdom and tips about life. Tips like the ones grandpa used to give him when he was young.

"Dude, you did a great job hitting the ball on your first day. I'm proud of ya, bro! We'll keep practicing and I know you'll get better every time."

"Yeah, it was pretty cool. I always thought golf was boring when I saw it on TV." Josh says.

"Hey, looks can be deceiving," Sidney says, "just like this neighborhood you and your mom live in. A lot of those people think that neighborhood is as far as they can go, but you have to understand that this place is not the end for you. There's a lot more in the world for you to see and do besides here." Sidney tells Josh as they pass through the neighborhood with vacant and abandoned houses with graffiti painted all over them.

"I know, my mom always tells me that. I told her one day I'm gonna get her out of this place and buy her a big house."

"Always take care of your mom. When no one else is there for you, your mom will be there. Help her out as much as you can. It's tough being a mom and single parent. The better you behave, the easier her life is. So stay out of trouble. I didn't have a dad in my life, only my mom to raise me."

"Wow, you don't have a dad?" Josh says. "I thought you probably came from some rich family! I don't know my dad either. My mom and Ms. Ella never talk about him. All I know is that he's somewhere in Louisiana."

"Rich family?" Sidney asks with excitement. "Man I grew up on a farm in a little town called Red Back and later moved here to New Orleans with my mom. But I had my grandpa and my crazy uncle Ray to guide me. Grandpa always told me to be the man of the house and make life easy for Mom. You gotta be the man of your house. That means doing stuff without your mom having to ask you to do it. Like taking out the trash, cleaning the apartment or calling to let her know where you're at because all moms worry about their kids. My mom still calls me even though I'm grown just to see where I'm at. But I love her, though. I don't know what's going on with your dad, but I'm here for you kid.

"I'm here for you if you need to talk about anything. Girls, life or whatever. See, I know there's some things you don't feel comfortable talking to her about since she's a woman. So my door is always open to you, kid."

Sidney and Josh pull up to the apartment and head upstairs. Josh opens the door and walks in, announcing himself and Sidney. "Mom, we're home!"

Denise has just finished washing her hair and has on a white fitted tank top, short running shorts and flip flops. Her hair is still pinned up. You can now see the truly petite hourglass shape that was hiding under her bulky work clothes earlier. She's naturally beautiful without any makeup and a body to match. Sidney notices, but he's trying not to stare at her. Since the last time he's seen her, she's come a long way from the industrious looking chef uniform.

"Did you guys have good time?" Denise asks as she walks into the kitchen.

"Yeah it was pretty cool."

Yeah, he's got a good swing. Golf might be his new sport," Sidney interjects.

"All right, baby. Go finish the rest of your homework that you didn't finish at the tutor's so I can check it. It's getting late and I want you to have some rest for school tomorrow. And tell Mr. Sidney thanks for hanging out with you."

"Baby?" Josh quietly asks his mom. He's embarrassed to be called that in front of Sidney.

"Oops, I'm sorry! Young man is what I meant to say." Denise says, correcting herself.

Josh looks at Sidney and says, "Thanks, Sidney. It was cool. Maybe next time we can go play a real game of golf."

"Sure, champ," says Sidney. "So after one day at the driving range, you're ready for the golf course? We'll see. Good night, little bro!"

They give each other a fist bump as Josh goes to his room.

Denise steps close to Sidney and says, "Hey, thanks for spending time with him. I can see he really had a great time. And I'm sure I probably would have never taken him somewhere like that. It's good for him to see he can do other sports besides football or basketball."

"No problem. Well, it was nice meeting you two. I'll see about getting with him next week. Okay?"

Sidney sticks out his hand to shake Denise's and she takes it and holds it.

"Sounds fine to me," Denise says in a seductive manner. She's still holding his hand and he's staring at her as though he's in a trance.

"Well ... I'd better be going."

"Yeah, and I got to help him with his homework," agrees Denise as she seems to snap back into reality. She opens the door and Sidney walks out.

Sidney is walking down the stairs talking to himself.

"What am I doing?" he asks himself under his breath.

Sidney is on his way home after a long day. He's ready to relax and spend some time with Karen and their daughter. Once he finally turns onto his street he sees his neighbor Sheila who lives across the street. She's struggling to get a large box out of the back of her red Mercedes. Looks as though she went to a store that has great prices on furniture but the tradeoff is you'll have to put it together yourself once you get home. Sidney sees her trying to lift the box, but it's obvious she can't. He pulls up and parks in his driveway. He hops out to jogs across the street to her rescue.

"Hey Shelia, let me help you with that!" he says as he makes it to driveway.

And to her surprise, it's Sidney. She instantly remembers what Karen told her about asking her Sidney to do anything.

"Oh, no… no … no … no ... I have it!" she says with nervousness in her voice.

"No. Don't hurt yourself! Plus, that's what neighbors are for!" Sidney says, insisting on picking up the box.

He goes straight to the box and picks it up with his manly strength with no struggle at all.

"Please…no! … I can handle it!" She says as Sidney starts walking toward her front door. She's walking backwards in front of him and sometimes behind him as he continues to walk toward the door like a man on a mission.

"Honey?" A voice says coming from a distance.

"Oh. God." Shelia immediately stops and mumbles while tensing up as she hears the voice come from behind.

"Hey, Sweetie, I was just pulling up and I saw Sheila trying to handle this big box by herself. So I thought I'd help out," Sidney says as he turns and holds the box with ease.

He explains to Karen as she's walking across the street from their house.

"Well, that's what neighbors are for!" says Karen.

"Hey! That's exactly what I told her!"

"I told him I had it! But he insisted," Sheila says in her defense.

"Oh that's alright. I know you need help … and my husband is a helper," says Karen sarcastically.

The three head toward the front door of Sheila's large house while passing her prized landscape. It's so meticulous that it's won the "lawn of the month award" a few times in the neighborhood. She has some beautiful, colorful flowers that look pristine and perfect enough to be on a magazine cover for gardening.

"Oh, those flowers are so beautiful!" Karen says, following up with "I've never seen them this close up!"

"Did your yard guy plant them like most people in the neighborhood?" Sidney asks.

"No. No. I did all of it myself," she says nervously. "I love planting beautiful flowers and gardening. It's a passion of mine."

"Well, you did a great job," says Sidney. "It's not too often you see flowers this pretty in November, so close to Thanksgiving."

"Thanks," Sheila says reluctantly.

Sidney makes it inside behind Sheila with Karen following behind him.

"Where do want this?" asks Sidney.

"Oh, right here is good enough."

"You have a beautiful home, Sheila!" Karen says.

"Thanks," she says rather reluctantly once more. "Well, thank you guys for helping me out. I'm not going to hold you up!"

"Hey, it was no problem," says Sidney. "I just hate seeing someone struggle when I know I can help out."

"Anytime you need something, just let us know."

Karen steps from behind Sidney to look at Sheila with a grin and evil eye. And Sheila notices it too.

"Sure thing! Well, thanks again. I'll walk you out," Sheila says as she ushers them to the door.

"Well honey, let's go eat," says Karen. "I've got dinner ready and we don't want it getting cold!"

CHAPTER 5
NITE TIME RUN

It's dinner time back at Sidney and Karen's house. The family is just finishing up.

"Honey, this salmon is great!"

"Well I'm glad you liked it, Babe! I put a light honey glaze on it," Karen says with confidence.

"So, what do you think about Sheila?" Sidney asks.

"Ally, eat your carrots sweetie," Karen commands their daughter.

"She's alright from what I see," replies Karen. "Why do you ask?"

"Oh, I was just asking. I wonder if she gets lonely in that big house all by herself with her husband always traveling," he says.

"So, you think we should get her a dog?" Karen says with sarcasm.

"What? A dog?" he asks, confused. "No, I was just thinking maybe you could hang out with her. You know, just be neighborly or do some neighborly things."

"Like what?"

"You know, like go get coffee, shop or just hang out with her. No one should be lonely around this time of year."

"Umm, I don't really know her. All I know is that she's into flowers and yoga classes. So, as you can see, we have a lot in common," Karen again says with sarcasm.

"Well, anyway, I was just thinking we should be neighborly."

"So glad you're on this community outreach campaign, Sidney! First, you start mentoring a poor kid of a single mom. Now you're worried the lady across the street might be getting lonely in her big house while her husband travels around the world without her. Hmm, maybe we should buy some shoe inserts for the crossing guard so her feet won't be hurting."

"Umm, I just don't know where this conversation is headed so I'm gonna work in my office for a little bit," Sidney says as he's trying to leave the conversation.

"Ally, baby, finish your dinner and get ready for bed. It's getting late." Karen tells their daughter.

"I'll be in my office." Sidney says.

"You know what? I think I'm going to go for a run tonight around the block."

"This late?" asks Sidney

"Baby, it's only 7:40 And I'll be carrying my pepper spray if it makes you feel comfortable."

After dinner is over, Karen loads the dishwasher and goes upstairs with Sidney to tuck Ally in bed. Afterwards, both head downstairs. Sidney goes back into his office to work. Karen gets ready for her night time run, She put on her running clothes, which includes a black hooded sweat shirt, and heads out through the laundry room. In there, she has refillable water bottles. Some are small bottles and some are large thirty-two ounce bottles. She reaches for a thirty- two ounce bottle, but instead of filling it with water, she fills it with bleach and heads out the door.

****

The next day, Sidney is at the office with Howard. They're on a call with a long-time wealthy client, Mrs. Jackson. They've put her on speaker phone so they can look at papers and talk to her at the same time. While on the call Sidney gets a text and it's Denise. She's texting to thank Sidney for spending time with Josh.

"Yes, Mrs. Jackson. If you can get us the receipts for your daughters' tuition, I'm sure we can get your taxes decreased and help you keep more money in your pocket." Howard says into the speaker.

"That sounds good to me. And Sidney how is that wife and beautiful daughter of yours?" Mrs. Jackson asks.

They're doing great," he replies while looking down at his phone as it's vibrating again. It's Karen, and she's sending a dirty little text message about what she's going to do to him tonight when he gets home.

She does this frequently to keep the spice in their marriage and make sure it doesn't fizzle out like a few of their friends' marriages have done recently.

"Well that's great to hear. I need you to take care of them, Sidney. Don't be like that old buzzard I just divorced after 30 years of marriage," says Mrs. Jacksons voice from the speakerphone.

Howard pushes the mute button. "Well, if you keep your big account with us he can take care of them for the rest of their life. You are just soooo fine Ms. Jackson! Those sexy hips and that nice round...ughhh and you're rich too!"

"Will you stop playing and unmute her?" Sidney demands.

Howard continues to joke around while Mrs. Jackson is talking and the speaker phone is muted.

"Dude you see how beautiful she is for sixty? Put me in the will, Mrs. Jackson. Leave it all to me!" Howard continues with the phone on mute.

Sidney's phone vibrates once more. He looks at the text and it's Denise again. Her text says, "I need your help with school project."

Mrs. Jackson is still talking and Sidney decides to quickly return Karen's text message. He tells her how he can't wait to get home and have his way with her. He unmutes the phone as Mrs. Jackson seems to find a stopping point in her longwinded talk about her divorce.

"I'm sorry about what's going on with you and Mr. Jackson. But don't worry: Karen and I plan on being together forever."

"Well, I'm glad to hear that Sidney," she says. "It's good to see young couples happily together and not dealing with all this of drama and crap we see on TV. Oh well, I'm heading to a meeting with my real estate agent. She's showing me some houses since I'll be getting a new one from the divorce. So I'll have to talk to y'all later. Oh, and Howard?" she says unexpectedly.

"Yes ma'am?"

"When you learn how to work the mute button on a phone, I might put you in my will."

Howards face drops and looks flushed as Sidney looks at him, shaking his head. Mrs. Jackson laughs and hangs up the phone. "Dude, I thought the button was muted!" Howard says with amazement and shock.

In the meantime Sidney gets a text back from Denise.

The text reads, "Oh, really? What do you think your wife will say about us doing that?"

Oh, no! Sidney sent the wrong text to Denise. Unbelievable, he sent a dirty text to Denise, thinking that he was replying to Karen. The usually cool and laid back Sidney puts his head down on the table in disbelief of the boneheaded mistake he made.

"What's your problem?" asks Howard. "I just sent a text to Denise that was meant for Karen.

"So what's the big deal? Just tell her you sent it to the wrong person."

"It was a very, very, very private text." Sidney says.

"Ohhhh, one of those texts…huh?

Didn't you just meet her yesterday? And she already knows your freaky side. Bro, you moving kinda quick on that one, aren't ya?" Howard jokes.

"I'm not trying to move on her at all! I sent the message to her by accident!"

"Wow!" Howard says. "So … how do you clean that up? That's an awkward situation. How does she look?" he asks.

"She's very beautiful, but that's beside the point," Sidney replies. "That has nothing to do with this."

"Well, I don't know exactly how you married people do it, but I'd say you probably need to forward your dirty little message to Karen since she's probably wanting a reply and wondering where it's at."

"Man, you married people!" Howard says as he leaves the conference room.

Sidney is sitting alone by himself at the table. He forwards the correct message to Karen. Next he sends a message to Denise saying, "Hey, I'm sorry for the text I sent you earlier. Please understand that I didn't mean to send that out. My stupid phone is acting up," Sidney writes with an attempt to fix the situation.

Denise replies back and says, "Oh really? I'm so disappointed! I was thinking we could go down to the courthouse today and get married. Then we could do all of those things. Dang it! Missed out on another one!"

Sidney looks at his phone with a dumbfounded look.

A few seconds later another text comes in from Denise. It says, "LOL! Just kidding! No problem! We've all sent some text that we didn't mean to send. But do what you need to do and keep your wife happy. Thanks again for spending time with Josh. Later!"

Sidney sits back and laughs it off and gets ready to walk out of the conference room.

There's some loud voices coming from outside in the form of an argument. It's two of the contractors arguing again. It's usually the result of one person getting in the way of the other since Sidney and Howard gave them a tight deadline to get the office remodeled. But Howard is there to break up the argument and Sidney chooses to stay out of it and head toward his office to get his stuff. He's leaving for the day. He has to visit a client later and then he's off to spend some quality time with his wife. He's got a hot date tonight with Karen at a new restaurant she's been wanting to try out, and then a passionate night at home afterwards. He asks Deb his secretary on the way out, "Did you make reservations for tonight at the restaurant for me?" She gladly replies, "Yes, sir. Have fun!"

In the meantime, Karen is at home upstairs in her bedroom window looking across the street at Sheila's house. She's holding her cell phone and smiling at the dirty message Sidney sent back to her. She loves this man dearly and will do anything to keep him happy. She wasn't too happy with seeing Sidney help Sheila out yesterday. It's about time for Sheila to leave for her daily yoga session as she normally does about this time. Karen knows this because she keeps an eye on Sheila to make sure she's not a threat. Sheila's looks can be intimidating with her long model legs, Serena Williams butt and Jennifer Aniston smile. Right on time as expected, Sheila comes out the front door headed to her red Mercedes convertible parked in her driveway. She's talking on her cell with one hand and holding her gym bag in the other. She briefly glances at her award-winning flowers while passing by.

Then, unexpectedly, she stops right in front of her car before walking to the driver side. She drops her bag and her phone as though she's been paralyzed.

She turns and looks back at the flowers. She screams and yells out, "Nooooooooooooooooo!"

Oh, no! Her beautiful flower bed that was filled with vibrant reds, bright yellows and electrifying purples is now rotten brown like a bad banana. She runs over and gets on her knees with tears in her eyes to examine them. She can't figure out for the life of her, what happened.

Karen is viewing this entire scene as it happens right across the street from her upstairs bedroom window. Without remorse or guilt, she simply says, "I warned you."

CHAPTER 6
MOTIVATION

Denise has had a long day at work and she's headed to her night class. She's tired, worn out and relieved that she's almost finished with school. She's recently discovered motivational and inspirational CDs. She listens to them daily on her commute. She's really entrenched in the CD she's listening to now.

"So maybe life has not been fair to you so far! But you have the right and authority to change your life from here on out," the man on the cd says.

Denise is deeply tuned into every word and feels empowered by the CD.

"You had some things go wrong that seemed like life was headed in the wrong direction. But today you're going to turn it around!" says the speaker with authority.

While listening to the CD, Denise is stopped at a red light across the street from a park. Her attention is drawn to a family of four consisting of what looks to be a father, mother and their two kids; a little boy and a baby girl. The father is teaching the boy how to throw a baseball while the mom and baby girl are sitting on a blanket watching them and laughing.

"If you can see it, you can achieve it," the man yells from her car speakers.

Life hasn't been fair to Denise. Her mother committed suicide when she was a baby. She doesn't know her father. She only has a picture, which has been ripped in half as the only clue of her father. The faded picture has a mans tattooed arm wrapped around her mom and was taken at an old night club. Her son, Josh's father, abandoned her when she was four months pregnant. It's obvious she's had some obstacles to overcome in life. But she's determined to continue fighting to have a better life for herself and for Josh. There's only one thing missing. A man.

A man to stand beside her as she thrives and reaches for success. She needs someone to help guide her son and show him how to be a real man. She's never had the love of a real man. That's one of missing elements of her life. But there's a new man in her life that seems to possess everything she's been missing. He's both a family man and successful businessman. He's tall, good looking and he smells great.

"Today is the day your destiny changes because you're taking control of it," says the speaker on the CD.

****

It's dinner time. Sidney and Karen are at the new restaurant that has just opened. Karen's been hearing a lot of good things about this upscale restaurant from her friends. They're enjoying the live music from a house band that's playing smooth, relaxing jazz. The restaurant is dimly lit by the candles at each table. The wine list is superb and the staff's attention to detail is impeccable. There's a well-dressed gentleman walking around the restaurant greeting guests to make sure they are receiving superb service. At some tables, he holds small conversations with the patrons to show appreciation for their business. His suit is custom-tailored and worn with a crisp clean white dress shirt with silver cufflinks. He seems to be a man of style; he's well put together.

"How's your steak?" asks Karen.

"It's tender and juicy. The chef did a great job!" Sidney replies as he enjoys the perfectly-cooked, medium-steak.

"So, Honey, how's the mentor program going? You haven't told me anything about it. All I know is you disappeared for a few hours last week and that's it."

"He's a good kid. His name is Josh. He has his head on straight, but just needs someone to motivate him to do well in the environment he lives in," says Sidney.

"Oh, okay! I'd like to meet him sometime. Maybe he can hang out with us and Ally one day.

"I'll talk to his mom. I'm sure she'll be cool with that," Sidney replies.

Sidney's phone starts to vibrate as a text comes in. It's Denise. Sidney looks down at the phone and tries to keep calm as he reads the text which says, "I want you. I want you now!"

"Who's that?" Karen asks as she takes a bite of her steak with part of her attention focused on the live band.

"Oh, it's just some auto text from a telemarketing company. Instead of calling now, they annoy you by sending texts." Sidney replies with his quick and unplanned answer.

"So tell me about his mom. Does she have any other kids? Is she one of those welfare moms?"

"No. "She's holding it down as best she can. Josh is her only kid. She works a job in the day time and goes to cooking school at night. She's a single mom and Josh's dad is a deadbeat."

"Oh, wow! We both know how tough that can be since you and I are products of the same type of home," says Karen.

Sidney's phone vibrates again. He looks down and sees it's Denise texting him again. He doesn't read the message.

"Hey, I've got to use the bathroom. Can you tell the waiter to refill my water glass if he comes by?" Sidney is itching to talk to Denise and tell her to stop what she's doing.

"Sure, Honey! Don't be long. I don't want your food to get cold!"

Sidney gets up to head to the restroom. He pulls out his phone once he's inside the restroom. He looks at it to finally read the second message. It says, "Hey, I'm sorry, I sent that to the wrong person. I guess you're not the only one with slippery fingers."

Denise sent the message as a payback to Sidney from earlier that day, when he accidently sent her a dirty message that was meant for Karen.

The phone rings and it's Denise on the caller ID. Sidney is hesitant to answer. As the phone's ringing, the man in the tailored suit who's been going from table to table greeting guests, walks into the restroom. Sidney never paid him any attention while in the dining room and this is his first time seeing the gentleman. As the man enters the restroom, he greets Sidney, "Good evening, Sir!"

"Hey, how's it going?" Sidney replies as his phone is still ringing and he waits for the gentleman to pass by.

The man is doing a gentle wipe down of the restroom making sure no paper towels are on the floor and no water spots are on the marble counters.

Sidney finally answers his phone on the fourth ring.

"Hey, what's up Denise?" Sidney says.

"I'm am such a dummy for sending you that message!" says Denise over the phone.

"No problem. But, can you not send me texts after hours? That's when I'm usually spending time with my family."

There's a pause on the phone and Denise hasn't replied.

"Umm ... sure," she says. "I'm sorry. I hope I didn't disturb you."

"It's okay," replies Sidney. "I probably should have told you earlier."

"Well, I will let you go and get back to your family, and again, I apologize. Hey, when you come by next Thursday, I'll have something special for you and your family."

"You'll have something special for me?"

"Yeah, a little something I've whipped up that I know you guys will love," she says.

"Well, hey, I've got to go. I'll see you next Thursday."

The man in the tailored suit is still wiping down the bathroom to make sure it's as meticulous as the dining room. Though he's cleaning, it's hard not to hear Sidney's side of the conversation on the phone. He's looking at Sidney's reflection in the mirror as Sidney's back is turned while he's on the phone.

He's silently grinning as he hears bits and pieces of a conversation that appears to be a married man having an affair on his wife.

Sidney steps up to a urinal to use the restroom. When he's done he goes to wash his hands and the man in the suit is gone.

Sidney finally makes it back to his table where Karen is anxiously waiting.

"Hey, are you alright? Didn't expect you to be gone so long. I thought I may have to come in after you," she says.

"No, everything is fine. The band is sounding better and better as the night goes on," Sidney says as he's trying to steer the conversation in a different direction.

After greeting other dinner guests the man who's been going from table to table, finally makes his way to Sidney and Karen's table.

"Good evening, folks. I'm Lawrence, one of the owners, and I just wanted to check on you to make sure you're enjoying yourselves!"

Karen is looking surprised and blurts out, "Lawrence!"

"Karen?" he replies back with no hesitation.

She stands up immediately and the two hug. To Sidney's surprise, Karen is now hugging the guy who was just cleaning the bathroom.

"Oh, wow! I haven't seen you since graduation! Sidney, this is Lawrence. He's the reason I passed calculus in college."

Lawrence greets Sidney with a grin on his face. From what he's overheard in the bathroom, Sidney is cheating on Karen with some lady named Denise.

"Well! Nice to meet you, Sidney!"

"Same here," says Sidney.

"This is so great! I cannot believe our paths have crossed again after all these years, Lawrence!"

"I remember us staying up all night studying together. You'd go home to take a nap and I'd go straight to class in the morning so I wouldn't forget anything. I didn't even brush my teeth. I just wanted to go straight to the test. I'd be praying that nobody would want to talk to me so I'd take off right after the test."

"So that's why you would run straight to the dorm after a test and never would talk to anyone?" Lawrence asks.

"Yep! I had to run off and brush my teeth!"

They both laugh while Sidney is still trying to figure out this situation. He and Karen went to different colleges after high school. Karen has never mentioned Lawrence to him. Karen invites him to have a seat at their table.

"So I guess all that studying definitely paid off for you! You own this?" Karen asks.

"Yeah. Myself and my partner. We're getting ready to open up another one across town next month and one in California right after that. And I definitely want you guys to be my special guests at the grand opening across town."

"Oh, we'll be there to support you, especially if it's as nice as this one! I don't see a ring on that finger so I guess you're not married yet?"

"Naw, not yet. The restaurants have me busy and I'm staying in a hotel while I'm here. I'm always looking, though! You got any friends?

"You're still crazy, I see," Karen says.

"So Sidney, what do you do?"

Sidney starts to speak but is interrupted by Karen. "Sidney runs an accounting firm with his business partner. And because of that, I can stay at home and take care of our daughter," she says.

"Oh, that's cool. I may have to talk to you about helping us get our books together. You have a business card?"

"Sure, here you go," Sidney says as he's reaching for his wallet.

Lawrence takes the card and slips it into his coat pocket.

Lawrence grabs Karen's hand, in a friendly way, while looking into her eyes and says, "Karen, it was great to see you again. I'll give Sidney a call and we can hook up sometime."

Sidney is looking at Lawrence's hand as he's holding Karen's. He's somewhat annoyed by the display of affection between the man he just met and his wife.

Sidney, jumping in quickly, looks firmly at Lawrence and says, "Yeah that sounds like a plan."

"Lawrence, what are you doing for Thanksgiving? It's only in two weeks away?" Karen asks.

"We're actually closed that day, so I'll just be hanging out at my hotel taking the day off," he replies.

"Nonsense! We're having family and some friends over and I want you to come hang out with us. I insist."

"Well, sure. If it's okay with you, Sidney," Lawrence says as he looks to Sidney for approval.

"Why not?"

"In that case, I'll definitely come by and hang out with you guys since the restaurant will be closed." says Lawrence.

"Hey, since you helped me out in school, I'll take care of your bill tonight!" Lawrence says with appreciation.

"Lawrence, you don't have to do that!" both Sidney and Karen say at the same time.

"Denise, it would be my pleasure!"

Lawrence has accidently called Karen, Denise. Sidney immediately looks up at him while trying to hide the shock his body is experiencing. His temperature goes up and he's feeling the heat. He realizes Lawrence must have overheard his conversation in the bathroom on the phone with Denise.

"Why did I just call you Denise, Karen? I better stop drinking on the job and dealing with so many different waitresses!" Lawrence says as he tries to clean up his mistake.

Karen just looks at Lawrence with an odd stare and nods her head as he tries to move the conversation forward.

"Well anyway, it's the least I can do for all your help, and I know we'll probably be calling on Sidney for some accounting work. Hopefully, this will help me get some kind of discount!"

"Umm, sure. Why not?" Sidney says half-heartedly. He's still thinking about how this guy just called his wife Denise.

CHAPTER 7
THE LOVE RIDE

Karen and Sidney are picking up their SUV at the valet stand, heading home for the night after their wonderful dining experience at Lawrence's restaurant.

"Wow! That was fun. I'm glad we got to check it out. The live band was great!" Karen says.

"You never told me about Lawrence or staying up all night with him," Sidney casually mentions.

Tilting her head and looking surprised, she inquired, "What's to tell? He was a friend from college. I helped him and many other students, which was a requirement to keep my scholarship. I don't think I know all your friends from college, do I?"

"Well, I'm keeping an eye on him. I noticed the way he was holding your hand."

"Sounds like somebody is a little jealous ... and that turns me on! Look, I'm a happily-married woman, in love with my childhood sweetheart, who is a wonderful husband, father, provider and lover. You and I will be together for the rest of our lives." she says while putting her hand on Sidney's thigh.

On their way back home they pass a lake that's nearby. It's a beautiful fall night with the moon reflecting off the calm lake water. It's late and the usually dark night is illuminated by the light of the moon.

"Turn right at the next entrance," Karen says unexpectedly.

"What?" Sidney replies, sounding surprised at the out-of-the-blue request.

"Just turn right up here into the lake. It's so beautiful at night," she says.

Sidney obliges and does what he's told. He turns into the lake off the busy street. He follows the winding road that circles the lake for about half a mile at a calm cruising speed.

Karen tells him, "Pull over here."

He pulls to the unpaved side of the road. As soon as the SUV comes to a complete stop, Karen takes off her seat belt and jumps into Sidney's lap, straddling and kissing him passionately. Karen deeply loves this man and will do whatever it takes to make sure he's happy and doesn't feel any threats about their marriage.

****

A few days later, Sidney is pulling up to the apartments where Josh and Denise live. He's picking up Josh to go hang out and do something fun like go-cart riding or bowling. After parking, Sidney goes upstairs and waves to Ms. Ella as she's sitting on her downstairs balcony, just like last time. He makes it upstairs and knocks on the door and Denise answers.

"Hey, how's it going?" Sidney asks Denise as she opens the door.

"It's going good. Josh is running late. He's at track practice and he's got another hour before it's over.
 Didn't I text you?" she asks.

"No, you didn't," Sidney replies.

"I could have sworn I did. Oh well. Anyway, I made something for your wife and daughter. She hands him a tin of homemade pastries filled with cookies and brownies.

"Hey, you didn't have to go out and buy this. The people at the store are going to be upset that you bought their stuff and made it look as though you made it." Sidney says jokingly.

"Buy? Are you for real? You know I've been going to school for the last two years to be a pastry chef and you think I'm going to buy you desserts? I don't buy desserts! I make desserts! I make masterpieces for your information."

"Is that so?" Asks Sidney.

While drying her hands after washing them in the sink, Denise tells Sidney, "Do me a favor and close your eyes."

"What?" Sidney asks with a confused look.

"Just close your eyes. I want you to do a blind taste test and tell me which tastes better." She says.

Sidney notices two bowls on the table with mixing spoons in each bowl.

Sidney reluctantly says, "I guess." and closes his eyes.

"Now tell me which one of these icings taste better. Number one or number two?" Denise says.

She sticks her finger in the small bowl of icing. She then takes her finger and puts it up to Sidney's face.

"Open your mouth," she commands, then sticks her finger, covered with icing, into Sidney's mouth.

He's surprised and opens his eyes. He had no idea she would use her fingers.

"Well, what do you think?" she asks.

"I like it," Sidney says.

"Now, try this one," Denise says as she's dipping her other finger into a mixing bowl to get icing. She puts the other finger in his mouth with the 2nd icing.

Now while this is going on between the two of them, Ms. Ella is coming upstairs to drop off some pots she borrowed from Denise.

As she's about to knock on the door, she can see Denise and Sidney through the blinds. They're standing in the kitchen with Denise's finger in Sidney's mouth. She stares through the window and shakes her head. Then she turns around and heads back down to her apartment.

Back in Denise's apartment, her cell phone rings. It's Josh calling from track practice. He's ready to be picked up. Denise tells Sidney that they'll have to finish this taste test later. Since it's getting late, Sidney plans on coming back another day to pick up Josh. He leaves the apartment with the homemade cookies and brownies for his wife and daughter. As he's leaving, he passes by Ms. Ella's apartment. She watches through her front window as he drives off. She's eager to get upstairs to confront Denise and goes into the apartment without knocking.

"Denise what are you doing?" she says with disappointment.

"I'm making a cake and I'm about to go get Josh from practice!"

"No, Denise. What are you doing with Sidney?"

"I'm not doing anything with Sidney!"

"Look Denise, you're playing with fire. I might have cataracts, but I ain't blind. I see what's going on here.
Look, he's a good man. But he's also a married man. Baby, you don't need to be messing with a married man!
I know I raised you better than this."

"I'm not messing with anybody Ms. Ella!" Denise shouts.

"Look, Baby, I just don't want you to get hurt and turn out like your momma. God rest her soul."

With tears in her eyes, Denise replies, "My momma? Oh, so you think I'm going to be like my momma and kill myself! And leave my child without a parent over some man because he didn't want to be with her?"

"I'm sorry, Baby. I know I shouldn't have said that," Ms. Ella says as she realizes her mistake. She had good intentions but her delivery was bad.

"Do you know my pain? Do you know my pain?" Denise asks with a stern voice. "My mom's been dead since I was two months old. I've never had a dad to hold me and keep me safe late at night when it was thundering and lightning outside or when I heard a creepy noise. I never had a man to say to me, 'Baby it's all right. daddy's here.' All I have is a picture! A picture! A ripped in half picture of my mom with a man's arm around her. I never told you, but I used to sleep with that picture at night. I used to see other little girls with their fathers and I'd be so embarrassed that I didn't have one. I used to tell kids in school that my dad was in the army and that's why he's not around. I felt so lonely. I deserve to be happy. I deserve to have a good man in my life. I have a beautiful son that's without a dad just like I was. And that's not fair to him just like it wasn't fair to me. Please don't ever tell me that I'm going be just like my momma. Because I'm not!"

"How could you say something like that?" Denise shouts with tears streaming down her face.

Ms. Ella goes to hug and hold Denise and says, "Baby I'm sorry! I shouldn't have said that. Look, I just don't want you getting hurt, chasing after a married man. I raised you and you're the daughter I never had. Baby, you don't have to take some other woman's man. God's got a man for you and Josh. And he doesn't belong to anyone else but you. You just wait and see. Baby, don't be one of these home wreckers out here that messes with married men so you can say you got a man. You're smart, pretty and I know you'll be a success with your baking business. You cook so good that you had that man eating out your hands, literally!" Ms. Ella says jokingly.

Denise looks at her and laughs with tears still in her eyes. The two ladies embrace with a long hug.

Sidney left the apartment and is on his way home. While driving, his mind is on Denise. Her cute face and beautiful body. Her witty sense of humor. More so, her body. He's admitting that there is a physical attraction. Part of him says, "Hold on. You've never cheated on your wife before." He starts to think back on what his grandpa told him when he was boy. Grandpa said, "Always take care of your family and stay with your wife for life."

Another part of him is saying, "Go for it! One time won't hurt. She's probably wanting the same thing. Howard does it all the time. She's probably just wanting something physical so you won't have to worry about anything long-term. Just do it!"

He starts talking to himself out loud and says, "Don't do anything stupid. You have a beautiful wife and daughter at home."

But he can't help but think of Denise. There's an attraction there that he hasn't felt in a long time.

"Get it out your mind," he tells himself as he pulls up to his house.

CHAPTER 8
THE BRAWL

It's a new day and Sidney is just getting into his office. There's an important client meeting this morning and he wants it to go perfect.

"Don't forget, the people from the Whitlow Corp. will be here at 9:30 a.m. sharp. They called and confirmed late yesterday." Sidney's secretary says as he's coming into the office.

"I got it. I'll be ready." he replies. Sidney and Howard have been trying to do business with this large corporation for a long time. After months of prospecting and calling them, they've finally arranged to meet with Sidney and Howard. If the Whitlow Corp. agrees to do business with them, this will be a huge multi-million dollar contract. Sidney's studied everything he could find out about the company. He knows their weaknesses and strengths. He's got thirty minutes before they're due to arrive and he's deeply studying some last-minute notes when he gets a text from Denise.

The text says, "Hey, you! How are you on this fine morning?"

Sidney types back, "Fine, thanks for asking. Kinda busy now."

"I hope your wife and daughter liked the brownies and cookies I made for them. I put a little something extra in them," the text says.

"Brownies and cookies?" Sidney thinks to himself.

It takes a second for him to remember. He remembers bringing in the tin, but he didn't give it to Karen. He sat the tin on the entryway table where he normally puts his keys as well.

"I'm sure they like them. Will text you later," Sidney writes, as he lies to get rid of Denise.

"Ok," replies Denise in her text message.

She sends another text message shortly after and it annoys Sidney as he's prepping for his big meeting. This time the message from Denise says, "Are you at your office?"

Annoyed by this question, Sidney replies, "Yes, and very busy!"

Denise sends back another message with a photo attached that says "Hope this helps your day go by quicker."

Sidney thinks to himself it's probably some little motivation picture or happy face.

Sidney clicks on the attachment and his eyes get big. Denise has taken a picture of herself wearing a spaghetti-strapped tank top and boy shorts and sent it to Sidney.

He stops everything he's doing. His mind goes from the important meeting with the Whitlow Corp, to being mesmerized by this photo.

"Oh ... my ... God," he says to himself in disbelief. The photo of her cute face, curvy body and those boy shorts have Sidney weak at the knees and he has to sit down at the conference room table.

Out of nowhere comes some noise. There seems to be some crashing, thumping noises along with screaming and yelling. This is bad timing! The Whitlow Corp. will be arriving shortly and they don't need to hear any disruptions in the hallway. Especially something as childish as an argument. Sidney decides to step out of his office to see what's going on.

"Look, my guy was here first! You're gonna have to work around us!" Luis screams.

"No! We were here first today. We've been here since 6:30 this morning!" shouts Melvin as he's holding a two-by-four in his hand.

These arguments have been going on since the start of the remodeling project with these two contractors and their crews. They've come very close to getting physical but luckily they haven't got to that point. Neither one of the men seem to notice Sidney heading their way.

As he is walking out of his office, he sees Luis holding a broom stick as a weapon and Melvin is holding a two-by-four. As Sidney quickly intervenes to break up the argument, Melvin turns around.

****

It's a Saturday morning and Sidney is asleep in his bed after a long and busy week of meetings.

"Daddy wake up! Mommy's cooking breakfast, then you're taking me to the zoo, remember?" Ally says as she's jumping into her parents' bed to wake up her dad from a deep sleep.
"It's time to go! The zoo is going to be so fun!"

Waking up from his deep sleep, he tells her "alright princess! Give me a minute to get ready. Let me get up and get dressed, then I'll be down."

"Okay, Daddy!" Ally says as she kisses him and jumps off the bed to go downstairs.

Sidney's feeling his head while in bed. He's got a headache and heads toward the medicine cabinet in the bathroom.

Sidney is coming downstairs for breakfast as Karen is setting his plate on the table. She walks over to him and gives him a good morning kiss.

"Morning, Baby!" he says as Karen hands him a cup of coffee.

"Morning, Sweetie! You slept like a log last night. You were snoring like a chain saw. I know you'll have plenty of energy for the zoo today with Ally."

"I can tell from her excitement she's ready to go. I hope this headache goes away soon."

"Well, Baby, did you take something for it?" Karen asks.

So are you forgetting to tell me something about Denise?

Sidney's face gets very pale. His body temperature immediately rises and sweat starts beading off his head in a matter of seconds. His head was hurting before and now it's throbbing as he thinks about how he's going to get out of this one.

Looking puzzled, Sidney says, "Like what?"

"Like how good Denise bakes? You didn't tell me she was a pastry chef. You only told me she worked at a restaurant. Those cookies and brownies she made for us are delicious! I think I might gain 20 pounds if I eat that whole tin you brought home. It was hard, but I only ate one chocolate chip cookie and closed the tin back up."

Relieved, Sidney says, "Oh, yeah. She's good at what she does."

****

Later that day Sidney's at the zoo with his daughter, Ally. They're having fun as he's spending good, quality time with her. They're on a merry-go-round when he gets a text from Denise. He looks down at it while on the ride and it says "Can you come by today around 6? I need your help with Josh. He's been acting up."

Sidney sends a text back and says, "At the zoo now with my daughter. Will come by later."

Denise sends back a text saying, "You're the best! Have fun with her, and thank you."

It's later in the evening and Sidney's had a great day hanging out with Ally. He dropped her off at the house and is on his way to Denise's apartment. For some reason unknown to him, he told

Karen that he was running by the office for a minute to get some papers and then he'd be headed back home. He doesn't know if he lied to her because it may, arouse a suspicion from Karen that he's spending more time with Denise and Josh than expected, or if he just lied to keep from having to go into details. He knows his wife. She always has plenty of questions and wants details.

Sidney is pulling up to the apartment of Denise and Josh. He goes upstairs and knocks on the door. Denise opens the door by just sticking her head around the corner and that's all he can see as he walks in.

"Hey what's going on? Where's Josh?" Sidney notices Denise is wearing more of those short running shorts and a fitted tank top showing her curvy but petite body.

"He's gone with Ms. Ella to the store. They're buying groceries for the food pantry where she volunteers. Afterwards they're going stock the food at the pantry. So they'll be gone for a while.

"So what's the problem with Josh?" Sidney asks.

"There's no problem. I just needed to see you and tell you how much I appreciate you. Josh's grades are really starting to improve and his behavior has definitely changed since y'all started hanging out.

"What?"

Denise moves in closer to kiss Sidney. He backs up at first but then gives in. The two are now standing in the apartment kissing as she starts to unbutton his shirt.

****

In the meantime, Karen is home with Ally and they're watching television on the couch. They're eating cookies and brownies made by Denise. While eating them, Karen finds a note at the bottom of the tin with lip prints on it. She opens the note and it says "Thanks for all you've done. My son now knows what it feels like to have a real man in his life. Can't wait to be alone with you for more one-on-one time.

"Wow mommy, these are good! That lady makes great cookies!" Ally says as she enjoying Denise's chocolate chip cookies. Karen's mind has been blown and she's in a state of shock. As she's reading it you can see the anger in her face.

"Mommy what's wrong?" Ally asks.

"Nothing Baby. Mommy's going to be right back. I have to go upstairs and get a pill for my headache. I'll be right back."

Before she goes upstairs with the note, she takes the tin of leftover cookies and brownies to the kitchen and empties them in the trash.

"Ok," Ally says as she's more interested in her movie and doesn't notice the tin gone.

Karen is upstairs in the master bedroom sitting on the bed. She starts crying. She calls Sidney's cell phone.

In the mean-time at Denise's apartment, Sidney's phone rings while he's in the shower. She pulls it out of his pants and looks at it. The caller ID says Karen. She answers the phone with a seductive, "Hello?"

Karen pauses, surprised to hear another woman answer her husband's phone. "Who is this?"

"This is Denise, Karen."

"Where is my husband?"

"He's in the shower. Did you enjoy the cookies and brownies?"

"Have you lost your mind? Put my husband on the phone now!"

"Like I said he's in … my shower."

Denise hangs up the phone and puts it on silent. She also deletes the last call from the call log. She continues to do this as Karen is constantly calling back to erase any trace of her calls. Sidney has no idea while he's in the shower.

****

Sidney is on his way home from Denise's. He's stunned. He can't believe it. He did it. He cheated on his wife. He got caught up in a moment of lust and desire and did it. Though it felt good in the moment of passion, the ride home is not what he thought it would be. The ride home seems longer while filled with guilt and shame.

His mind is flashing back to that day Grandpa told him about treating your wife right and taking care of her for life.

"Why Sidney? How could you let this happen?" he asks himself.

He broke the vow he made to his wife at the altar. He broke the vow he made to his Grandpa. He's also a part of that line of family members who've cheated that Grandpa talked about that day they were fishing. Now he's feeling disappointed that he fell into the trap of cheating just like uncle Ray.

As he turns onto his street and pulls into his driveway, there's a heaviness on his heart.

"Put on the winning face," he says to himself before he gets out to go inside. He's cleaned up and taken a shower at Denise's apartment to get her scent off him. He's already planning his next lie to Karen. She thought he was going by the office to quickly pick up some papers and he'd be back home on this Saturday night to spend time with the family. But he's been gone a little longer than planned.

Sidney finally gets the courage to get out of the Range Rover in the driveway. He heads inside and drops his keys as he normally does on the entryway table. He walks into the kitchen where Karen is sitting with a bottle of wine and her bible.

He has no idea that Karen's been calling his phone numerous times since Denise put it on silent. He's also unaware that she talked to Denise since Denise deleted the calls from the call log.

Sidney greets her with his normal, "Hey, baby!"

"Hello, Honey. Did you get your work done at the office?" she asks. "I called you, but got no answer." She says.

"Yeah, I needed to go work out and relieve some tension," he says as he continues to lie.

"You must have called while I was at the gym and my phone was in the locker," Sidney says, as he continues to lie to Karen.

"The gym?" Karen asks.

"Oh. Okay," Karen says sounding puzzled. "Is everything alright?" she asks.

"Yeah, Baby! Everything is just fine," he replies.

"Well, I guess you're probably hungry. I'll put your dinner in the microwave and warm it up for you."

"Thanks, Babe!" Sidney leans in to kiss Karen.

Before he can plant his lips on hers, Karen asks, "So, how cool is Denise?"

"What do you mean?" he replies.

Karen asks nonchalantly, "Is she cool enough for you to be taking showers at her place?"

"What?" Sidney says.

Again, calmly, nonchalantly, Karen inquires, "Is she cool enough for you to take a shower at her apartment?"

There's silence between the two as they stare at each other.

"Oh, I think this belongs to you," Karen says calmly, sliding the note to the end of the table.

Sidney walks over and picks it up. He reads it. He knows that she now knows.

"Oh, Baby, I'm sorry. I'm sorry. I'm sorry!" He walks over to Karen to hold her and she pushes him away.

Karen is visibly upset now.

"Get off me! Just because you took a shower at her apartment, you think you're clean enough to touch me? How the hell do you think you have the right to come home and put your hands on me after you've been with her? Have you lost your mind? I've been with you since we were teenagers. I cook, clean and take care of our daughter and you wanna do this to me? Are you crazy? I always prayed that the stuff that happened in your family would never happen to us. Your mother is always talking about your crazy uncle Ray and the women he fools around with and I always said 'God, thank you, for not letting my Sidney be like that.'"

"Baby, I'm sorry. I feel so bad. It was a mistake. She means nothing. You, Ally and I are a family and I don't wanna lose that!" Sidney exclaims.

"Get out!" Karen says with authority.

"What?" Sidney questions in shock.

 "Get out!"

"I'm not leaving. We are going to work this out. Please," Sidney says, begging.

Karen tells him, "I need some time to myself. Either you leave or I'm leaving and I'll let you explain to Ally when she wakes up why her mother is not home."

Sidney looks as though he's in a tight spot. He says, "Fine. I'll go. But let me kiss Ally good night."

Karen says, "Tell her you have to go out of town on business for a few days."

Sidney starts packing some clothes. When he finishes packing he walks down to Ally's room. She's sound asleep. He gently wakes her up to tell her he has to go out of town for a few days. He's trying not to cry as he talks to her. She's looking surprised but half asleep.

Sidney whispers, "Baby Girl…Baby Girl?"

"Daddy?"

"Baby, Daddy's got to go away on business for a few days. But I'll call you every day and talk to you, okay?"

"You have to leave now?" she asks, looking puzzled.

"Yeah, Baby. I need you to know something before I leave. Your daddy loves you more then you will ever know. Don't you ever think that I'll stop loving you. I'm proud to be your dad. I thank God that he gave me a sweet little girl like you and I'm going to always be here for you no matter what, OK?"

"Okay, Daddy," says Ally, wiping the tear from Sidney's eyes. "I love you."

Still whispering and trying to pull himself together, he says, "Sweetie, Daddy's gonna call you in the morning."

CHAPTER 9
LONELY ROOM

Sidney packs the Range Rover and pulls out the driveway. He stops at the end of his street and starts thinking, "I have nowhere to go." He's never been in this position. Finally he gets his thoughts together and decides to go to a hotel downtown nearby his office. He has a corporate account there that he uses when clients fly in and stay overnight. On the way to the hotel, he calls Denise several times and gets no answer. He leaves her an angry voice mail. He also sends a text. She doesn't reply to either the text or voice mail.

Sidney has checked into the hotel and heads up to his room on the eighth floor. He's sitting on the bed looking distraught. He looks at a picture of his family on his cell phone. His phone rings and it's Denise on the caller ID.

Sidney answers his phone with anger, "Hello!"

"Well, hello sexy!" she replies.

Sidney, sounding half angry and half in disbelief, asks, "Are you crazy? Are you stupid? Why would you put a note like that in that tin?"

Denise replies, "Wait ... wait ... wait a minute. I don't know who you think you're talking to! Have you lost your mind?"

Sidney tells her, "I don't ever want to talk to you again! Do you hear me?"

Denise replies, "Really though? Look here. She found that note. The picture ain't looking too good with her. Sidney, why are you fighting this feeling you have for me? I seen it from day one."

"Are you sick? Are you on some medication or something? Do you realize I could lose my family over this?"

"So what, Sidney? If your family was that important you wouldn't have been in my bed, now would you? And besides, you know you and I have some chemistry. You already have a daughter and I have a son. So if you look at it … me and you will have a complete family. What do you think?" Denise asks.

Angry and upset, Sidney yells, "Are you kidding me? I don't have any feelings for you Denise. It was just sex. I thought that's all you wanted!"

"What?" Denise replies.

"Get that through your head. I could care less about you. I don't want to be with you. I want to be with my wife and daughter."

There's a long, silent pause. Finally Denise yells out, "Really Sidney? I know we're supposed to be together. I'm sorry for what I did, but I know we're supposed to be together. You know we're supposed to be together!" She hangs up with anger.

Sidney is alone in his hotel room with his bag unpacked. He sits on the bed with his head in his hands and he's disgusted with himself. The feeling of guilt and shame is overcoming him. If he could just go back in time and undo the damage that's been done.

Thanksgiving is coming in a few weeks and he's thinking of how this could be the first one away from his family.

****

It's been a few days since Sidney has seen his family.

He's driving to his house to pick up his daughter. He's taking her to a barbecue at his mother's house.
He sees an expensive car in the driveway as he pulls up and gets out his car. The tag says "Delicious" on it.
He goes to open the door with his key and it doesn't work. He rings the doorbell. The door opens and to his surprise he sees Lawrence, Karen's friend from college who owns the restaurant they had dinner at a few weeks ago.

"Who told you to answer my door?" Sidney asks with anger.

"Hey, hey, hey … easy, fella. I'm just doing what your wife told me to do. And from what she told me it might not be your house too much longer after she found that note." Lawrence says in an attempt to push Sidney's buttons.

"What?" Sidney asks with surprise.

"Oops, I forgot how big my mouth can be," says Lawrence.

Sidney pushes his way past Lawrence through the front door.

"Where's my daughter at?" he asks.

"That's right Karen did tell me you were taking her to a barbecue today! Oh, by the way … that European support mattress you got upstairs … man I haven't sleep that good since I was a baby." Lawrence says to antagonize Sidney even more.

Sidney is upset and reaches to grab Lawrence by his collar.

"I don't know what's going on here. But when I figure it out I'm going kick yo…

"Daddy!"

Ally, Sidney's daughter comes running from upstairs. Sidney hears Ally coming and he lets go of Lawrence's collar. She finally sees her dad and she's overcome with joy. She runs to hug him.

"Daddy!" she yells out with excitement as she jumps into his arms.

"Hey, Baby Girl!!! I'm so glad to see you!" Sidney says as he's hugging and kissing her.

Karen is coming out of the kitchen. And walking toward Sidney with a stern look on her face.

Karen says in a demanding tone, "I know you're taking Ally to your mother's barbecue. But I need you to have her home by 7 p.m. We're going to drive to Lawrence's lake house tonight.

Lawrence is grinning and looking devilishly at Sidney as he stands behind Karen. "Hey, hey, hey man. Look, you can take all the time you need with your daughter. Karen and I will find our own way to pass the time. Besides, my lake house is not going anywhere."

Sidney just looks at the two of them with angst. He can't believe this is happening. His wife has another man in his house that he's worked hard for. It's only been a short time since Karen found the note from Denise. And she's already got another man in their home.

****

Sidney and Ally are on the way to the barbecue. Their conversation is about how much she misses her dad being at home.

"Daddy when are you coming home?" she asks.

It's a question that Sidney has a hard time answering. But he knows he has to give a good and comforting reply.

"Well, Baby, when Mommy and I fix our problems, I'll be back," he replies.

"Well, Daddy, I get scared at night when you're not home. I think there's a monster in my closet. And you're not there to check the closet for me."

Sidney is torn when he hears this from his little girl whom he loves to protect. He's feeling helpless by not being a home with her at night.

"Baby Girl, I want you to know I'm always here for you. Whenever you want to talk, you call me anytime you want just like you've been doing. But remember, even if you can't get in touch with me, you tell God to send his Angels down to protect you and he'll do it. Ok?"

"Daddy, my friends at school said that when their mommy and daddy had problems they never got back together and they each got new wives and husbands. Daddy, are you getting a new wife and is mommy getting a new husband?"

Oh, wow. Sidney never expected this heavy a question. It came completely out of left field. He pulls over to the side of the road and parks. He then turns to look back at his little girl setting in the back seat.

"Baby, your daddy messed up. But I'm trying my hardest to fix it with Mommy. I love you and your mom and I hate not being at home to tuck you in at night and read bedtime stories. But I promise I'll never stop loving my little girl no matter what. Ok?"

"Ok Daddy."

Sidney's phone vibrates and it's Denise sending a text message. He looks down and pays it no attention.

Sidney's made it to the barbecue at his mom's house. The whole family is there: aunt Earnestine, grandma, grandpa and crazy uncle Ray. Other people are there as well while card games and dominoes are being played. As they come through the gate in the backyard, Marcy, Sidney's mom is glad to see her granddaughter Ally. She runs to hug her with excitement.

"There's my sweet grand baby!" she yells out.

Ally is happy to see her as well.

"Granny!" Ally yells.

They hug and embrace. Grandma and aunt Earnestine are helping cook side dishes while Grandpa is on the grill with the meat.

"Sidney, bring me that plate of burgers for the grill!" Grandpa yells as Sidney has barely arrived and he's already giving him orders.

Sidney takes the plate of raw burgers to Grandpa. As he's walking toward him, he's wondering what Grandpa will say to him about cheating on Karen.

"Here you go, Grandpa." Sidney says in a nonchalant voice.

"So, something you need to tell me, Son?"

"Well, what's there to say besides I messed up?" Sidney says to get sympathy.

"Yep. You messed up. We talked about this way back on the farm."
It's obvious he's not having any sympathy for him.

"Well, the only way to fix the situation is to find a solution. You need to do whatever you have to do to get your family back together," Grandpa says.

"Look son, Thanksgiving is going to be here shortly. You don't wanna spend that away from your family do you?"

"No, sir." Sidney replies.

Uncle Ray walks up to Sidney and grandpa as they're talking.

"Daddy, he can't help it. He's one of us. The women love us," uncle Ray says with confidence.

"Shut up, Ray!" Grandpa says with anger.

"Now, this boy is gonna do whatever it takes to get his family back. Look, you don't taint his mind and tell him he can go out and just get more women. Because I know you, Son, and I know that's what you're gonna tell him." Grandpa says as he walks away taking finished meat inside.

Sidney is left by the grill with uncle Ray.

"Look nephew, I know Daddy thinks he knows it all. But he has to realize. You're human. You make mistakes. Karen has to understand that. Look man, you run a business, take care of her and your kid and every now and then some banging chick is gonna cross your path and test you to see how faithful you are. Y'all been married ten years and this is the first time you screwed up? Uh, nephew she should have gave you a medal for going this long. Couldn't have been me! I'm just saying."

Sidney looks at Ray and is not surprised to hear these words from a guy who's been with an innumerable amount of women.

Shaking his head with disagreement, Sidney repeats Grandpa's words, "Shut up, Ray."

****

Sidney is at his office and he's looking at family photos on his desk. He's feeling sad and down as he's longing to be with his family.

"Sidney, you have a visitor" his secretary buzzes in to say on the speaker phone.

"Who is it?"

"She says her name is Denise." The secretary replies.

"Tell her I'm in a meeting and I'll call her later."

"Yes Sir."

A few minutes later his cell phone rings and it's Denise. He rejects the call. Shortly after, she sends a text which is deleted.

"What is wrong with this chick? Why can't she get it through her head that I'm not interested in her?" Sidney ask himself as he sits alone in his office.

Sidney is working late tonight and is the last one to leave his office. He's walking to his Range Rover parked in the parking garage in the space that's clearly marked for his company only. As he gets closer he notices that it's scratched up. He knows who did it and immediately calls up Denise.

"What the hell's wrong with you? You know how much it's gonna cost to get this painted?"

"Umm, Sidney, I don't know what you're talking about. What happened?" Denise says with surprise.

"You know what I'm talking about! Stop playing games!" he yells into the phone.

"Well, well. Finally got out of that meeting, huh, Sidney?" Denise says sounding sarcastic.

Sidney steps back two spaces from his Range Rover and hasn't gotten in yet. He's yelling at Denise through the phone, getting more and more frustrated with her.

"Denise, you need to move on," he says.

"I'm late," she says.

"Late? What do you mean your late?"

"Don't play dumb, Sidney. I'm pregnant."

"No. No. No. Don't try to put that on me. I don't believe it. I'm not the dad."

"Oh, OK. So now I'm a 'ho? Is that what you're calling me?"

"I am not the dad Denise!" He yells into the phone.

"Well Sidney, if this is how it's gonna be, it is what it is. Oh and one more thing. That tie you wore today is really nice. It really brings out your eyes. I see you have a nice collection of them." She hangs up. Sidney is still in the parking garage and is visibly upset as he pounds the hood of the Range Rover. The alarm goes off. He gets in and throws his brief case in the passenger seat and closes his door with anger. Suddenly something is wrapped around his neck pulling his head tightly against the head rest. He's choking and gasping for air. Denise was hiding on the floor of the Range Rover behind the front seats with her petite frame. She's choking him with one of his ties and he's fighting for breath. Unfortunately she caught him already out of breath, since he was angrily yelling in the phone at her. He's trying to loosen his neck and awkwardly swing behind. But the more he fights, the tighter the tie gets making it harder to breathe.

As he's fighting for breath, Denise is talking to him calm and collected. She's in the backseat with her feet planted firmly against the back of the driver seat for leverage. Her hands tightly grip the tie which is wrapped around both her right and left fist. She's squeezing every ounce of oxygen out of his body.

"Sidney, you are not going to make a fool of me. This situation is about to get real. I've been hurt by Josh's dad and that was my fault. I was young and dumb. Now I'm a grown women and I don't play games. Remember, I make some mean desserts, but I'm also a marine, so don't get it twisted. Don't try to screw me over. I'm gonna be in your life forever whether you like it or not."

She suddenly lets go as Sidney begins to black out. She gets out of the Range Rover and casually walks away. Sidney is still gasping for air and is too weak and winded to chase her.

CHAPTER 10
TIFFANY BOX

It's Thanksgiving Day and Sidney is in his lonely hotel room. There's a huge televised Thanksgiving Day parade going on outside of Sidney's downtown hotel. He's sad because he's never been away from Karen or Ally on Thanksgiving. There's a large crowd gathering on the streets below and he's looking at them from the window of his high rise hotel room. Families are there having a good time with kids who are anxiously awaiting their favorite inflated cartoon characters and floats. He can see dads walking around and carrying kids on their shoulders. Something he used to do with his daughter.

Sidney's phone rings and he sees it's Karen. He picks it up with anticipation that she'll invite him to spend time with her and Ally on this holiday.

"Hey, Honey!" he says with excitement as though there's no issues in their marriage.

"Are you kidding me? Are you serious?" She replies.

"What are you talking about?"

"You know you really chose to have an affair with a psychotic and sick in the mind…piece of trash. You and her can go to hell! Do you hear me Sidney?"

"Karen I'm sorry! I'm going to fix this and we'll be back together!"

"Sidney do you know what Ally found on our door step this morning in a nice little blue Tiffany gift box with a bow tie?"

"What?"

"I opened the box and found a pregnancy test. A positive pregnancy test! She yells."

"Karen no! No Karen! That is not my baby. I would never do that to you.

"Really Sidney? You tell your sick and twisted new baby momma that if I ever catch her around my house again, we'll have to call the coroner to pick her up!"

She immediately tells him, "I need money. The car notes are due, the mortgage, electricity and everything else."

Taken back and surprised Sidney says, "Is that all you have to say to me? Karen, we've been together all these years and have never spent Thanksgiving apart, and now you treat me like I'm just a source for money? Can you show me some kind of respect? I know I messed up and I'm going to fix it!" he says.

"First of all, Sidney, we are not together. Get that through your head. You're my husband and I catch you sleeping with another woman, and you tell me to show you respect? Show you respect?"

"I'm not trying to argue with you. Where's Ally?"

"She's with Lawrence at the store getting some last minute stuff for Thanksgiving."

"What? Wait a minute! You let some man that I don't even know anything about go somewhere alone with my daughter?" Sidney yells.

"Some man?" Karen yells back. "Look, I've known him for a long time and it looks like he's really good with her. He took her to a basketball game last night with courtside seats and she had a great time. And besides, he and I are thinking about taking our relationship to another level."

Sidney is surprised.

"What's that supposed to mean?" Sidney asks with astonishment.

"Look, he's a good guy, and he's opening up a new restaurant on the West Coast and I'm thinking about moving out there with Ally to help him. And when we do, you can have the house and cars Sidney."

Sidney is blown away by what he's hearing. He can't believe how much damage has been done to his marriage because of one mistake.

"Are you serious? Karen, you can't be for real. Baby, I messed up. I admit it. Let's work this out. It happened just one time!"

"Sidney, all it takes is one time. One time to make a mistake that will change your entire life. I can't be with you knowing you've slept with another woman. I can't get it out of my head. And now she's pregnant?"

Frustrated, Sidney is standing up against a wall and he bangs his head on it.

"I don't believe this, Karen. I just don't believe this," he says.

"So, are you going to send the money for the mortgage and the car notes or what, Sidney?" Karen asks without a care in the world.

Sidney hangs up his phone and slams it on the bed. He then plops face first in bed next to the phone.

His phone rings. He figures it's Karen calling back. He rolls over to look at the phone. It's Denise. He just looks at the caller ID. He declines the call. It rings again. She's calling back. This time he answers the phone with anger.

"What do you want?" He yells into the phone.

Denise is crying and there's a noise of wind in the background. Like someone riding in a car with the windows down.

"Sidney?" She says with a sorrowful and pitiful voice.

Immediately after she says his name, another call is coming through. It's Karen on the other line. Sidney chooses not to answer Karen's call.

"Sidney, I know how you feel about me. And I'm sorry I never meant to hurt you." Denise says with a weeping voice and the wind blowing in the background.

Sidney is somewhat relieved. Denise is finally getting it through her head that he doesn't want anything to do with her."

Another call is coming in on the other line. Sidney thinks it's Karen but instead it's his mother.

Shortly after a text message comes in from two of his customers but he doesn't read the messages. He's more focused on fixing the Denise situation.

"Look. Denise! You're a nice woman. And I know there's someone special out there for you, but it's not me." Sidney says.

Another text message just came through but it'll have to wait.

"Thank you, Sidney." Denise says. "I want you to know that you'll never have to worry about me or our baby again. Will you please take care of Josh for me?"

Somewhat relieved, he's intrigued and asks her, "What do you mean take care of Josh?"

Denise hangs up the phone on him.

Immediately after he hangs up his phone, it rings and it's Karen.

Before he can say hello, Karen screams into the phone, "What the hell have you done?"

"What do mean? What are you talking about Karen?" he asked in surprise.

Several text messages are still coming to his phone one after another.

"Turn on Channel 7 now!" she yells into the phone.

Sidney turns on the TV and his eyes get big as he stares at the screen. He drops his phone and starts to throw up from what he sees. Denise is standing on the ledge of a high rise building along the Thanksgiving parade route. There's thousands of people below her on the ground who came to watch the parade. The parade has come to a halt because of Denise standing on top getting ready to jump.

A TV news anchor is reporting this breaking news. "Ladies and gentlemen we hate to interrupt our broadcast of this nationally televised parade, but apparently there's a lady on top of a building along the parade route who's threatening to jump with a crowd below," the reporter says.

"Police and firemen have cornered off a section on the ground below as the crowd has many children in it, looks up with amazement," the reporter continues. "If our helicopter can zoom in we can read what she has written on a neon green poster with black writing."

As the news helicopter zooms in you can see what Denise has written on the poster.

"OK, thanks for zooming in guys, it appears that the poster says, Sidney Rivers doesn't love me and our unborn child." The reporter says from the studio.

Sidney is still standing in front of the TV with disbelief and his hand over his mouth.

"Whoever Sidney Rivers is, hopefully he can get to this lady so this situation will end positively." The reporter says.

Sidney realizes the building is two blocks over from his hotel. He looks down at his phone on the ground.

He picks it up and Karen's still on it. Karen is still their yelling his name. "Sidney! Sidney! Sidney!" she yells.

It's still buzzing with text messages.

"I gotta go, Karen!" He yells into the phone and hangs up.

He looks at the large amount of text messages coming through. There's so many saying, "Turn to channel 7!"

One says, "Is that lady talking about you on the t.v?"

Another says, "Do you know the lady on top of the building on Channel 5?"

The text message from Sidney's mom says, "Baby, go get that girl."

Apparently several TV stations are reporting the story of Denise on top of the building since it's breaking news.

Sidney tries to call Denise back but the phone keeps going to voice mail. He decides to go get Denise down.

He rushes to get his keys and runs out of the room. He's in the hallway waiting for the elevator but it's too slow. So he takes the stairs and makes it to the lobby which is seven floors below.

He finally makes it to the first floor. As he swings open the stairway door it slams on the wall behind it making a loud noise that gets the attention of people in the hotel lobby. They're gathered around a large wall mounted flat screen TV, watching a news station covering the story. Some ladies are crying and holding their heads in disbelief. There's a family huddled in a corner praying for the lady on top of the building. Sidney just looks at them as he's running through the hotel lobby.
He overhears some people talking as he's halfway to the front door.

"I can't believe she jumped over a man," says one lady with tears in her eyes,

"God bless her soul, may she rest in peace," says one man as comforts a crying lady.

Sidney stops as he realizes what's happened. He's out of breath and bent over with his hands on his knees.

Denise has jumped from the ledge. Sidney starts biting his fist while trying to hold his composure around the group of people.

"Amazing how people will kill themselves for love," says one lady.

Then the lady at the front desk yells across the lobby at Sidney as he looks noticeably stressed and bent over like he's in pain.

"Mr. Rivers, are you OK?" she yells loudly.

"Hey! Wait a minute. Aren't you Sidney Rivers, the name on the sign she held up before she jumped?" yells the lady from the front desk across the lobby.

He looks at her and stares while still in shock and out of breath.

"You're the one she killed herself for?" says another lady in the lobby which has gotten very quiet with most eyes on Sidney.

"Wow, buddy, this is all your fault?" asks a guy who's with his family in the lobby.

Sidney says, "It's not my fault."

The front desk lady says again, "it's your fault!"

Sidney repeats, "It's not my fault!" But this time he says it loud with anger.

Then another man in the lobby says the same thing, "It's your fault!"

Another lady repeats the same thing.

Sidney is overwhelmed and starts screaming at them, "It's not my fault!"

All the people in the lobby are screaming. "It's your fault! It's your fault! It's your fault!"

Sidney starts screaming back at them" It's not my fault she jumped!"

"It's not my fault! You have to believe me! It was just one time!

****

"Sidney! Sidney! Sidney, wake up!" a voice is screaming out of nowhere.

Sidney's vision is getting blurry as he continues to scream, "it's not my fault she jumped!"

"Sidney you're having a dream! Wake up!"

"Wake up Sidney," the voice says with authority.

Sidney's eyes are slowly opening with confusion. He looks up and sees Karen and his mother. Karen's holding his hands. "Baby it's OK! I'm here. You're dreaming."

Sidney grabs her hand and sits up in a hospital bed with excitement.

"Baby, I'm sorry. Forgive me. Please forgive me!" Sidney says as he starts kissing her with excitement.

Sounding puzzled, she asks, "Forgive you for what? You must have been having some dream after getting knocked out."

Sidney looks confused. He questions her. "Knocked out?"

 "Yeah, you got knocked out!"

"You don't remember anything?" Marcy asks.

His mother tells Sidney what happened that lead him to being in a hospital room.

"From what Howard told us, you came out of your conference room to break up an argument in the hallway between your contractors, Melvin and Luis. As you walked up to break up the fight, you got hit in the head with a two-by-four, which knocked you out. The paramedics couldn't get you awake for anything, so they brought you here to the hospital. The doctor said you have a concussion. So you've been here at the hospital for the last three hours unconscious.

Sidney is overcome with joy as he's hugging and kissing Karen after learning he's been dreaming ever since he was knocked out. The only thing he can remember is walking up to a fight between Melvin and Luis. The affair with Denise was only a dream. Everything is fine with him and Karen.

"Where's Ally?" he asks.

"She's with aunt Earnestine and she's gonna be so relieved to know that her daddy is ok," Karen says.

****

Sidney and Karen are leaving the hospital and headed home. It's been a long day for Sidney, so Karen is driving. Plus his head is still pounding after being hit with the 2 x 4. "Hey, let me ask you something: what were you apologizing for when you woke up from your dream," Karen asks.

Sidney looks out the window and says " I was just apologizing for not being the best that I can be to you and Ally.

She looks at him and says, "Yeah ... OK."

Then she changes the subject. "Hey, you know those cookies and brownies you brought home from Denise?"

Sidney is drinking a bottled water and starts to choke in the middle of a swallow. He starts coughing violently.

"What is wrong with you!" Karen yells. Are you ok? Do we need to go back to the hospital?

"No honey. I'm fine! I'm fine! The water just went down the wrong way!" he says as he continues to cough and hopefully change the subject.

"Well anyways like I was saying before you started dying over there, those things are soooo good!" Look, you know next week we're having the family over for Thanksgiving. I'd love it if she could make all the desserts! You know the cakes and pies? You think she'd be willing to do that if we paid her?" Karen asks excitedly.

Sidney, sounding unsure, says, "I don't know. I'll have to ask her."

"OK. Well, give me her number and I'll call her today. You'll probably forget to call her," she replies.

Sidney still sounding unsure says, "OK."

Sidney is finally back home. He's glad to see his little girl. He hugs and kisses her as though he hasn't seen her in long time, even though he last saw her this morning before he left the house.

Later he's sitting in his back yard while Karen prepares dinner.

Sidney's still relieved that he was having a dream. A dream. A dream. He was able to see it all. Karen opening the tin. Lawrence in his house. Denise clearing his call logs. Denise being mean, crazy and choking him. It was all a dream! It's as though God was saying to him, "I'll show you how this is going to turn out if you keep going down this path." Getting hit in the head by that 2 x4 actually saved his marriage. Sidney's relieved that he hasn't cheated on Karen. Unless he calls letting Denise feed him icing with her fingers cheating. While thanking and praising God for a second chance, his phone rings. It's Denise.

He's reluctant to answer but he knows he has to set her straight on how their relationship will be if he's going to continue mentoring Josh.

He answers on the fourth ring.

"Hey, Denise, how are you doing?"

"I'm OK." Then there's a pause on the line.

"Hey, I need to talk to you about something!" both exclaim at the same time.

"Wow!" Sidney says, surprised they spoke in unison.

"Let me go first." Denise says. "Look, I want to apologize for what I did the other day when I did the 'blind taste test.' Hey, I'm really sorry for sticking my finger in your mouth. I didn't mean anything by that. I've been feeling uneasy and out of line about my actions ever since then. Look, you have a family and I'm not trying to be some hoochie momma, home wrecker. OK?"

"Yeah!!!" Sidney thinks to himself. He wasn't sure how she'd take it when he was going to lay down the line and set her straight. He didn't know if she'd start crying or go crazy like she did in the dream. Wow! What a weight off his shoulder! Now there's only one thing for Sidney to say.

"OK." he replies.

He continues, "Hey, look, you're right. I really shouldn't have let you do that anyway … even though those icings were both great."

They both laugh.

"I need to ask you something. Next week we're having Thanksgiving at our house. My wife really liked the cookies and brownies and wants to know if you would bake some desserts for us."

"Sure! I think I can do that … for a good price of course," she replies.

"Well … we were hoping you would do it for free."

There's an awkward pause on the line.

"Just kidding!" Sidney says with a laugh.

"You idiot! I thought you were being for real. I was thinking, 'Surely these people don't want me to cook for free?'" Denise laughed in relief.

"All right. I'll give my wife your number and you two can work that out," Sidney adds.

"OK, do that. I'd love to help her out. Well, I'll talk you later, Sidney. I've got stuff in the oven."

"OK, talk to you later."

Before he hangs up Denise shouts, "Hey, Sidney! Thanks again for helping Josh. He really appreciates the time you guys hang out. He says you're like a big brother to him. So … thanks again. OK?"

"Sure," he says, and hangs up.

Sitting beside his pool, Sidney looks up to the sky, holds up one finger and says, "Thank you, God!" Then he walks into the kitchen from the patio and tells Karen that Denise is fine with baking the desserts for Thanksgiving.

"OK, great!" Karen says as she passes by with a load of laundry. She heads out the kitchen and upstairs.

When she leaves, Sidney goes to the tin of brownies and cookies on the bar. He opens it and looks inside, pulling out the tissue paper. He wants to be sure that there's nothing in the tin besides cookies and brownies. He's relieved to find no notes with any message. "Hey, it never hurts to be sure," he thinks to himself.

He doesn't notice Karen stopped at the top of the stairs. She turned back and looks down at him. She curiously stares at him while he pulls out the tissue paper, but doesn't say anything, she simply continues on her way.

****

The next day, Karen calls Denise to tell her what she wants baked for Thanksgiving.

"Hello." Denise says as she answers.

"Hello Denise, this is Karen. Sidney's wife. How are you doing?"

"Ah Karen! I've been expecting a call from you. Didn't recognize this number. I'm doing fine, thanks!"

"Well, you know why I'm calling. I need to know if you can bake some cakes and pies for Thanksgiving with our families coming over. Your cookies and brownies were so delicious!"

"Well thank you! Sure! I can do some baking for you! What did you have in mind?"

"Oh, something good. Like 7-Up cake, German chocolate, lemon pound cake and, of course, some sweet potato pies are always great to have.

Oh, and one more thing: I love cheesecake! Can you do it?"

"I sure can! That's one of my specialties!" Denise says excitedly.

"OK, great! Now that that's out the way, let me ask you a question. Are you sleeping with my husband?" Karen asks with no hesitation at all.

There's an awkward silence on the phone. Denise is shocked and somewhat paralyzed by the upfront and boldness of the overprotective, "nobody is taking my man" Karen.

Though she wants to scream, "Are you out of your freaking mind asking me that question?", Denise calmly replies, "No, I have no intentions to sleep with your husband or you. And if you think I'm going to be a part of some kinky stuff y'all are practicing, I don't want any part of it."

Karen didn't expect that response in a million years. Now, she's in a state of shock herself.

"OK. Let me explain something to you," Denise says. "I don't know what Sidney has told you about me.

Maybe you're thinking I'm one of those single moms who are lazy and desperate for a man, any man, married, single, divorced etc. Well let me tell you myself, about me. I work a full-time job and provide for my one and only son, with no assistance from a man or the government. I served as a marine in both Iraq and Afghanistan.

When I have a flat tire, I don't call roadside assistance. I get out and change it myself instead of waiting on a man. When I go to work and get a paycheck, I can say I earned it and it's my money. I don't depend on a man who can pull the rug from under me at any time and I'll have nowhere to go with no money. I go to school full-time at night and will be graduating in one month with a culinary chef degree specializing in pastry baking. So I really don't have the time to get caught up with the drama of being the other woman. And when God sends me the right man, I'll be the only woman. And I'll be secure enough in myself and my relationship that I won't have to go around asking other women are they sleeping with my husband."

Karen is floored and doesn't know how to respond. Nobody, nobody has ever read Karen her rights like this after she did what she calls one of her "protect your marriage" moves. Karen has no choice but to humble herself and flat out apologize.

"Look, Denise, I'm sorry. I apologize. I was wrong for asking you that. From what I've heard, you're a good person. You have to understand as a wife I always want to make sure no one is trying to take my husband."

"I understand Karen, but there's a way to go about that without disrespecting another woman."

"Denise, I'm sorry if I've made you uncomfortable. I understand if you don't want to make the desserts for me."

"Karen, I'm a tough woman. I've been through a lot in my life. And I still go through a lot being a single mom. But I'm strong and I don't let anything like that bring me down. I'll be glad to help you out. I'll try to drop them off on Thanksgiving eve so you'll have them fresh for Thanksgiving Day."

"Well, what are your family plans for Thanksgiving?"

"Not too much. My son Josh, and I will probably spend it with my godmother who lives in the apartment below."

"That's it? No other family?"

There's an awkward silence. Overbearing, big mouth Karen has spoken without using her brain, again.

"Well, actually, no." Denise replies. "See, my mother died when I was two months old and her best friend, Ms. Ella, raised me. Ms. Ella never got married or had kids of her own so she was like the only mother I've had in life. I don't know where my father is or even if he's alive. But you know what? I'm happy with this little family we have and I know with me going to school and graduating next month, things are only going to get greater from here."

"Denise, why don't you, Josh and Ms. Ella come have Thanksgiving with us?" Karen asks.

"No, don't feel you need to have us over because I've told you my life story," Denise replies.

"No, Denise that has nothing to do with it. Now, I've never met you in person but I can see you seem to be a genuine person and I think we can have a good long-term friendship. Plus, I want to meet that nice son of yours that Sidney has told me about. I'd love to have your family over. Please accept?" Karen asks, again.

"OK. We'll do it. We'll spend Thanksgiving at your house and I'll bring over the desserts then."

"Oh, great. And I'll have a check for you. I can't wait for you to meet the rest of our family. I'm sure they'll take a liking to you guys. I'll text you the address. We'll get started around three o'clock, but if you could make it a little earlier, that'll be great so we can have everything already set up," Karen says.

"Sounds like a plan."

"Well, great! It's all set. I'm texting you the info now. We'll see you next week! And Denise, thanks for setting me straight on some things today."

"I'll talk to you later, Karen." Denise says as she hangs up.

****

It's finally Thanksgiving Day. Everyone is looking forward to celebrating at Sidney's house. Grandma and Grandpa are driving up along with uncle Ray and aunt Earnestine from the family farm in Red Back. Uncle Ray usually likes to bring one of his girl friends to the family get-togethers but this time he had no choice but to leave them since there's little room in the car with the dressing and turkey that grandma has smoked.

Sidney's mom, Marcy, is coming by shortly since she lives only fifteen minutes away. Denise, along with Josh and Ms. Ella, will arrive early as she and Karen planned. Denise has been in the kitchen preparing her gourmet desserts since last night and she finished a few this morning. As requested she's made a variety of cakes and pies, including a sweet potato pie, that has extra nutmeg in it to take the flavor up a notch.

As they're driving in Sidney's neighborhood, they can't help but notice the large pristine houses with neatly-manicured lawns.

"Wow, Mom, these houses are big!" Josh says from the back seat.

"They sure are. Look at that one with a four-car garage," Ms. Ella adds.

"That's OK. We'll be here one day y'all when I get my dessert business off the ground," Denise says positively.

As they pull up to Sidney's house, they see it's just as nice as the others in the neighborhood. They unload and head to the front door. Josh rings the doorbell, which Karen answers with a large smile on her face.

"Well you must be Josh!"

"Yes ma'am."

"And you're Denise."

"Well, yes, I am! And this is my godmother, Ms. Ella."

"Well come on in, I'll show you where the kitchen is," Karen says.

Denise and Ms. Ella are truly impressed with the inside of the house. They're scoping it out and taking it all in while they follow Karen into the kitchen.

"Sidney should be down any minute. He's upstairs taking a shower. You can set the cakes on the bar and the pies on this counter here."

Denise is in awe of the kitchen. It's truly a chef's kitchen with plenty of space, stainless steel appliances and granite countertops. It's nothing like her kitchen at the apartment where it's sometimes tight when both she and Josh are in it.

"Wow! You have a beautiful kitchen," Ms. Ella enthuses.

"Oh, well, thank you. It's a tough job keeping it clean, but I do it myself even though most of our neighbors hire maids," Karen says, trying to find common ground with her guest.

"Mommy can I have a snack?" asks Ally as she comes around the corner from the living room. "I'm hungry!"

"Well, who is the pretty little girl with those pretty bows in your hair?" asks Denise.

"Aren't you the sweetest little thing?" Ms. Ella says.

"Well, Baby, tell them your name!"

"I'm Ally and I'm seven years old."

"Hey, who is this guy in my house?" Sidney says jokingly as he's coming downstairs.

"Oh, don't do that to him, honey!" Karen says, sticking up for Josh.

Sidney walks over to shake Josh's hand and pats him on the back.

"So … if I become a drug dealer like you, I can get one of these houses too?" Josh says to get back at Sidney.

"Daddy, in school they tell us to stay away from drug dealers." Ally chimes in.

Sidney just shakes his head while looking at Josh. "Josh, I've told you before, leave the jokes to me."

"Ms. Ella, how are you doing?" Sidney asks as he walks over to greet her, giving her a hug.

"I'm doing great, Sidney. Thanks for inviting me along with Josh and Denise for Thanksgiving."

"It's no problem. Our house is your house. You guys just make yourselves at home just like family.

Speaking of family, I think my mother is pulling up right now. Hey Denise, do you have anything else in the car I can send Josh out to get?" Sidney says to joke with Josh.

"Yeah. I've actually got two more cakes and I made some more brownies like last week," Denise says.

That's something Sidney is not too comfortable hearing about. But regardless, he has to act as though he never had that dream which involved, of all things, brownies.

"OK. Come on, Josh, let's go get it. And I know my mom brought a few things as well."

"I'll help you guys," asserts Ms. Ella.

"No. No. Ms. Ella, you just hang here and relax. We'll handle it.

Sidney and Josh go out to Denise's car to get the rest of the pastries. They greet Sidney's mom, Marcy, just as she's getting a large pan of dressing out of her back seat.

"Momma, let me get that," Sidney chides.

"Oh, Son, I got it."

"No, Mom. I know you worked all night at the hospital and came home to fix this today, so I don't want you doing anything else today but relaxing."

"Well, you'll get no argument from me on that one," Marcy replies gladly. She inquires, "And who is this handsome young man?"

"Mom, this is Josh. He and I are in the mentoring program. I'm basically supposed to keep him from dropping out of school and becoming a convicted felon."

"What?" Josh says with amazement.

"Oh, shut up Sidney! I know a good kid when I see one."

"I'm just kidding, Mom, he's a good kid. He just needs someone to knock him around when he starts going down the wrong path.

"Well, nice to meet you Josh! And you don't pay him any attention. I had to knock him around a few times when he was about your age."

"Oh Ma'am, please tell me more!" Josh says with sarcasm to get back at Sidney.

"Well, Momma, just go on in. We got this stuff." Sidney says shutting his mother's car door and handing the dressing to Josh.

"Hold this like your life depended on it."

"All right, honey, I'll see you inside," Marcy says as she starts walking to the front door behind Josh.

Back inside the kitchen, Karen is helping set up the cakes Denise brought over as well as some of the dishes she prepared. Karen is checking out Denise without her noticing, as women do, but seldom admit to it.

She notices how pretty Denise is as well as her curvy, petite body. She's definitely attractive. Though she had a conversation with her last week about Sidney, she can't help but feel be a little jealous of Denise's looks. She's surely going to keep an eye on her without it being noticeable.

"Hey, Mom! Come on in! I see you've met Josh!" Karen says as Marcy enters the house with Josh behind her.

"Everyone, this is my wonderful mother-in-law, Marcy." Karen announces as she walks out the kitchen to greet her.

"Nice to meet you, I'm Denise and this is my godmother, Ms. Ella," Denise says while cutting slices of cake.

"Pleasure to meet you all," Marcy says.

"Well, Mom, you get off your feet and rest. I know you're tired," Karen orders Marcy.

"She's a nurse at the hospital and she works overnight. She got off this morning and insisted on fixing the dressing afterwards to make sure it was fresh." Karen explains to her guests.

"Oh, you must be tired!" Ms. Ella exclaims.

"I'm fine. It's not like I make dressing every day. Thanksgiving only comes once a year and I want to make sure we have the best dressing possible," explained Marcy.

Outside, Sidney managed to load up the two cakes along with the brownies from Denise's car. While heading inside he sees Grandpa, Grandma and Aunt Earnestine pulling up in a car driven by Uncle Ray. Sidney is surprised that Ray didn't bring any of his crazy girlfriends like he normally does at family get-togethers. Sidney can't wave since his hands are full but he smiles and nods his head to acknowledge them before he goes inside.

"Hey everyone, Grandpa and Grandma are pulling up with Aunt Earnestine and Ray," he says while coming inside.

"Josh, will you please help Sidney with the cakes?" Denise yells across the room.

Josh is somewhat amazed by the big TV Sidney has in the living room. He's taken in by the football game and the enormous size of the screen. Comparing this TV to his at the apartment is like comparing night to day, David to Goliath, Neiman Marcus to Family Dollar.

"Did Ray bring one of those crazy girlfriends with him?" asks Marcy.

"Didn't see any, Mom," replied Sidney as he sets food on the counter.

"Oh, thank God," says Marcy as she loads the dressing into the oven to warm it up. "I heard about two of them getting into a fight a few days ago at the Fish House. Apparently he forgot one was a waitress there when he brought another in on a date. My brother," adds Marcy, nodding her head.

"Wow. Sounds like he's a playboy," Denise says.

"Yeah, but it's time for that playboy to hang up his player's hat. Going around embarrassing our family!" Marcy says with disgust.

"Now who is that?" Marcy says with amazement as she's passing by the large kitchen window that looks out to the front yard and driveway.

A tall, handsome man is getting out of an expensive car. He looks well-polished in his shined Italian loafers, nice jeans, long sleeved, v-neck sweater and tie. His designer sunglasses are hiding his eyes.

Marcy, Denise and finally Ms. Ella make it to the window. The well-polished gentleman is crossing the street and coming up the driveway to Grandpa's car, helping him with a load of dishes Grandma has cooked. Grandpa gladly shakes the guy's free hand after handing off the food to him. Now he can help grandma out of the front seat while Ray loads items from the trunk. Aunt Earnestine pats him on the back instead of making him struggle to shake her hand. She follows behind him as he's walking toward the front door. She looks at the kitchen window and notices a few shadows standing there. Without the guy noticing, she looks at the window and winks along with a thumbs up for approval behind his back with her one free hand. Karen finally makes it to the window.

"Oh guys, that's Lawrence!" says Karen before going back to preparing food. "One of my college friends. He has a restaurant in town and we invited him this year since they're closed today. He's a really good guy."

Aunt Earnestine's jumped in front of Lawrence to open the front door and she gladly announces herself when she comes in.

"We're here, everyone! And look at this gorgeous man I've brought with me!"

"Oh stop, Earnestine! I can tell by his blushing you're embarrassing him," says Marcy.

"Hello, everyone," Lawrence says as he's walking toward the kitchen.

"Where can I put this, Karen?" he asks.

"Just set them right here on the counter, Lawrence.

Everyone, this is Lawrence. We went to college together … a long time ago."

"Well, nice to meet you Lawrence!" shout several others, including Denise.

Grandma is coming through the door with some help from Grandpa.

"Hey Grandpa and Granny! Come on in!" Karen says as she greets them and takes their coats with a welcoming kiss.

Uncle Ray finally enters and announces himself. He doesn't even ask where to put the dishes he's carrying, he just drops them anywhere in the kitchen.

"Where's my nephew?"

"Oh, I think he's upstairs in the game room with Josh," Marcy replies.

"Josh?"

"Oh, yeah, let me introduce you Ray, to Denise. Josh is her son and Sidney is mentoring him in a Big Brother program," Karen says.

"Well, since y'all can't make a boy, I guess that'll have to do!" Ray says jokingly about Sidney and Karen not having a son. But no one laughs. Most just shake their heads.

"Oh shut up Ray! They'll have a boy when they are good and ready." Grandpa says as he's heading toward the upstairs game room, asking, "Hey, Lawrence, you wanna head up to the game room with us while we let these women finish in the kitchen?"

"Sure!" Lawrence replies.

Grandpa, Lawrence and uncle Ray head upstairs to Sidney's game room which consists of another large TV with a football game playing on it, a pool table, a foosball table and a video game system that he rarely plays.

"Gentlemen. Gentlemen!" Grandpa says as he enters the game room.

"Hey, Grandpa!" Sidney says as he walks over. He shakes his grandfather's hand and gives him a pat on the back.

"Lawrence! You made it!"

"Yeah I did!" he replies. Thanks for having me over Sidney."

"No problem, man," Sidney says.

"My crazy uncle Ray! Hey, man, I heard about that incident at the Fish House!"

"Don't worry about that, nephew. There's two sides to every story," says uncle Ray in his own defense. "I'll have to tell you about it later."

"Hey guys, I want you to meet Josh. I'm his mentor in a program here in town," Sidney explains.

"Hey, what's going on? Nice to meet you, young man!" the three men say as they greet Josh.

"Are you any good at pool?" Uncle Ray asks Josh. "Because I've been beating Sidney too long and I need some new competition."

"Umm, I've never really played before. But I'm pretty good at learning fast. And then I'm usually the best at whatever sport I play." Josh says with confidence.

"Man! Cocky young guy, huh?" uncle Ray responds. "Let's get started." He walks over and gives Josh a pool stick and they go to the table on the other side of the large game room.

"Oh there's nothing wrong with the young man having confidence," Grandpa says as he's walking over to the couch in front of the TV.

"Sidney, I've always wondered about these mentor programs," Lawrence says while they're at the bar where Sidney's pouring a soda for himself.

"It's pretty cool. I've had some fun with it while helping a kid out and making sure he stays on the right path."

"Well, I'll have to get the contact info before I leave here," Lawrence replies.

While the guys are upstairs, the ladies are downstairs in the kitchen finishing up with the food preparation.

"Now who made this lemon cake?" Grandma shouts. "Oh, whoever did this knows what they're doing! This cake is so good!"

"Granny, Denise made all of the desserts. She's in school right now to be a pastry chef and she'll be graduating next month," Karen explains.

"Baby, this is so good! You can probably teach the class. You've got the right amount of extract in there and some natural lemons. I can tell," approves Grandma.

"Yes, Ma'am. I tried my best," Denise says humbly.

"This is really good!" Grandma says as she takes another bite.

"So, Denise, tell me about yourself. I already know you can cook! Is your family from around here?" she unintentionally pries.

"Well, I live with my son Josh and Ms. Ella here is my godmother. She's raised me since I was a baby. My mother passed when I was a few months old."

"Oh. Well, from what I see you seem to be a fine young lady. And I want you to know anyone who's a friend of Sidney and Karen is family to us. So any time we get together, you, Ms. Ella and Josh are always welcome." Grandma says to welcome Denise and comfort her after finding out about the rough circumstances of her life.

"She's right. So you consider yourself family!" Marcy exclaims.

"Well, the food's ready," says Karen. "Call the guys down so grandpa can bless the food."

"I'll go get them," Denise says while drying her hands on a towel. "Josh has been bugging me about coming upstairs to see this game room that he seems to adore."

"Yeah, it's Sidney's pride and joy!" laughs Karen.

Denise heads upstairs to the game room to get the guys. When she does, she stops in the doorway and the guys are unaware of her presence. She just stands there checking out the game room before announcing herself.

She sees Sidney, Lawrence and grandpa focused on the football game. Lawrence has gotten her attention and she can't wait to ask Karen about him. Sidney is yelling at the TV as though the players can hear him.

Josh and Uncle Ray are at the pool table and glancing at the game in between their shots. Josh seems to be having a good time. Denise is really glad to see him around a good positive group of men, which he rarely has the opportunity to do. She enjoys seeing the smile on his face as he's really gelling with uncle Ray. He's talking a little trash on the pool table as though he's been playing for years, even though she's sure this is his first time. Uncle Ray, with his shirt sleeves rolled up, can't help but to laugh at the young cocky kid.

Then it happens. Denise loses her breath and has to cover her mouth. It's like her body has gone into a state of shock and her knees are weak. She quickly ducks to the side of the doorway and covers her mouth. She starts to wonder, "Did I just see what I thought I saw?"

When she looked at Uncle Ray playing pool with his shirt sleeve rolled up, she saw the exact tattoo that's in the same place on the arm as the picture that she has at her apartment. The picture that she's had for years of her mother and a man's arm wrapped around her shoulder. The picture that her mother tore in half from anger, leaving only a man's arm with that tattoo on it just like Ray's. That arm in the picture is all she's ever known about her father. She had no face, no body, and no smile to go by. Only a picture of an arm.

"OK. Get yourself together," she whispers to herself.

She's got to talk to Ms. Ella since she was there the night her mom met this man with the tattoo, the night Denise was conceived. She composes herself and steps back into the doorway.

"Hey guys, the food's ready downstairs," she announces softly.

The guys are happy to hear this. Sidney puts the TV on pause so they don't miss any part of the game. They start heading downstairs and Denise is still in the doorway. She's examining uncle Ray's tattoo as he going through the doorway.

"Well, looks like I'll have to finish beating you after we eat!" Josh tells uncle Ray while behind him.

"Oh Josh, be nice!" Denise says, trying to make sure Josh is respecting his elders.

"Oh, he's ok. He's really picked up the game fast! And really, I'm letting him win to make him feel good," uncle Ray explains.

"What?" Josh says with surprise.

Downstairs everyone is gathered around in a circle holding hands. Grandpa is blessing the food. While everyone has their eyes closed and heads down, Denise is peeking at uncle Ray's arm. Then she peeks at Ms. Ella in hopes to get her attention. But Ms. Ella never looks up. She's properly praying, with her head bowed and eyes closed.

"Amen!" Everyone says at the end of grandpa's prayer. After that, everyone got their plates, fixed their drinks and went for their favorite dishes. Denise makes her way over to Ms. Ella as fast as she can.

"I need to talk to you!" she whispers in a serious tone.

"Is everything ok?" She asks.

"No. Well, yes. I mean … I just got to talk to you!" she says, still whispering.

"Ella! Denise! Come on! Eat!" Grandma yells across the kitchen to the two of them standing in a corner.

"We're coming!" Denise says, managing to muster up a smile.

"I think it's him!" Denise says with excitement.

"Him who?" Ms. Ella asks.

"My father!"

"What?"

"Look at Ray's arm. He has the tattoo that's just like the one in the picture with my mom and the man's arm around her."

Ms. Ella looks over at Ray across the room in the kitchen. Her eyesight isn't good enough to see that far.

"Well, look. Let me get a closer look and ask him some questions. But that was thirty- one years ago. We need to know for sure before we make a scene. And you can't just walk up to him and say, 'You're my father.' So just give me a few minutes to pick his brain, and I'll let you know what I think," Ms. Ella replies to a nervous, yet excited Denise.

"OK. Just do what you can," Denise responds.

Ms. Ella joins everyone in the kitchen while they are fixing their plates. Josh is helping Sidney's daughter Ally fix her plate. He's helping her out as a big brother would, while Karen, being a good hostess, makes sure everyone else has all they need.

 Lawrence has been checking out Denise and is asking Karen about her.

"So who is that with the jeans and red sweater?"

"Oh, that's Denise. She's a friend of the family. Sidney is mentoring her son."

"Oh, really? Sidney was just telling me about that upstairs."

"Yeah. She's actually in the same business you're in. She's going to culinary school and graduates next month. She specializes in pastry. As a matter of fact she made all of the cakes and pies here."

"Wow, she made that cheesecake? I haven't tasted a cheesecake that good in a long time."

Karen's matchmaker instincts kick in. She starts to think maybe she can hook up Denise and Lawrence. They're both single and in the food business. Plus, it's another way of keeping the very attractive Denise from moving in on her husband.

But while Karen is thinking about matchmaking, Lawrence is thinking to himself, "Where have I heard that name before? Denise?"

Then he puts two and two together. Denise was the name he overheard Sidney talking to on his cell phone in the bathroom at the restaurant. He remembers how Sidney was saying "I'm with my wife and don't call me this late Denise."

Lawrence thinks, "Sidney's having an affair with Denise and he's supposed to be mentoring her son."

"You know what? I think you guys would make a great couple. I'm gonna hook you up!" Karen says and walks off before Lawrence can agree or disagree.

"Hey don't!" he exclaims. But it's too late since Karen has taken off. She's actually walked over to Sidney and they start talking. He can't hear their conversation. But it's obvious, she's telling Sidney about hooking him and Denise up. Sidney looks at Denise. And then he looks at Lawrence and nods his head as if he's saying,

"Yeah, I guess they'll make a good couple but I'm gonna kill this dude if he's trying to move in on my side piece."

Karen walks off and goes to talk to Denise.

Lawrence is thinking to himself, "This isn't good. Karen's trying to hook me up with the woman her husband is having an affair with."

Then he considers it a bit more. "She seems like a nice lady. She's definitely attractive. And we've been looking for a pastry chef for our restaurants. Even if that's all I'd need her for. But, I'm not trying to get caught up in any drama messing with Sidney's mistress. I've gotta fix this before it gets out of hand."

Sidney has fixed his plate and is heading back upstairs to watch the game in his game room. Lawrence decides to follow behind him. But he's stopped by Sidney's mom, Marcy.

"Lawrence why haven't you fixed a plate?" she inquires.

"I'll get something shortly. I had a late lunch before coming over."

"Oh, that's nonsense! You need to eat! Come on. Let's get you a plate.

Unknown to Lawrence, Marcy also is trying to hook him up with Denise. She overheard the story when Denise was talking to Grandma about her being single. And she heard about Lawrence being single as well. Marcy thinks these two would make a great couple. She doesn't know that Karen has also talked to Denise about a potential connection between her and Lawrence.

Marcy takes Lawrence's hand and starts leading him over to stack of plates by Denise. "Denise have you met Lawrence?" she asks.

"Um ... I've heard some good things about him," Denise says uncertainly.

"You know what? I've got to use the bathroom. I'll be right back." Lawrence says to get out of this. He then heads upstairs to talk to Sidney, finding him in the game room with a plate of food watching the football game.

"Hey, Sidney! I'm glad I caught you!"

"Karen told me about you being interested in Denise," Sidney says. "She's a good catch. Smart. Funny. And she's not bad-looking either. Plus Josh is a good kid, too."

This is really starting to mess with Lawrence's mind. He's thinking, "Sidney is cheating with Denise and now he wants to hook him up with her? Is this dude crazy?"

"Hey look. I don't know what Karen told you. But I'm not planning anything with Denise."

"Why not? She's a nice girl, man!" Sidney asks.

Lawrence is fed up and decides to let it all out.

"Hey, look, I'm not trying to get involved with anything sticky. I overheard your conversation on the phone with her while you were talking in the bathroom. And I'm not trying to get involved with that."

"Wait … wait …wait. Are you thinking I'm having an affair with Denise?

"Hey, Bro. All I know is what I heard. I'm not trying to disrespect you in anyway."

Sidney just looks at Lawrence with disbelief, tilting his head to one side. Then he does something Lawrence never expected. He starts to laugh.

"Dude! I'm not having an affair with Denise. Look she's hot and cute and smart but I'm happily married to Karen. So she's all yours. You have my blessing if that's what you're looking for.

"Hey, I'm sorry. I probably should leave," says Lawrence sheepishly.

"Naw, it's cool! I probably shouldn't have been so harsh with her on the phone that night. But anyway, man, go for it. You're single. She's single. Go for it!"

Downstairs, Denise is sitting closely by Ms. Ella and Uncle Ray. She's eavesdropping on their conversation, but gets interrupted by both Karen and Marcy. They're still trying to hook her up with Lawrence. She's definitely attracted to him, but now is not a good time for that. She has to find out if uncle Ray is her dad.

"So Ray have you always lived down in Red Back?" inquires Ms. Ella.

"Yep pretty much all of my life, I've lived there. It's a nice little town. It's not too fast like New Orleans. It's a nice and easy town.

"Ray, that tattoo is neat. Looks like you've had it a long time?"

"Yeah, it's the only one I got. Funny thing about it, I got it when I was drunk."

"Oh, wow! Did you design it yourself or did you pick it off the wall at the tattoo shop?" If it's an original or one of a kind, then Ray is Denise's father.

"Nope, it's not original. It was on the wall with a lot of other tattoos to choose from. This one just jumped out at me.
I've actually seen a couple of guys with it over the years. He says with confidence.

Denise is starting to feel really let down now. She's almost at the point of crying. Why does this have to happen to her: getting her hopes up thinking she may have found her father?

I lived here in New Orleans just for a little bit, then I moved back to Red Back to help out my Dad on our farm," Ray says, eating while talking.

"Oh, really? How long ago did you live in New Orleans?"

"Oh, I guess it was about twenty, thirty … thirty five years ago. I can't remember exactly."

"Really?" Ms. Ella says. "Hey, did you ever hang out at that place over on 8th street called the Brick House?" she asks. "I remember around that time period, that was the happening spot."

"Umm, I don't remember the place. Doesn't ring a bell. You know, there was a lot of spots back then. There was the Fall Out Club, the Red Connection, Annie Mays, Tuckers…and the list goes on.

"Oh, no," Denise thinks to herself. He was a party guy who went to a lot of clubs. How could he remember what happened at one club? Especially if he's the player that the family is saying he is. He doesn't know if he's been to the place where her mother and Ms. Ella were hanging out. She's starting to feel deflated and let down, like she got her hopes up for nothing.

Ray are you sure you've never been to the Brick House Club?

"Hey, you know what? Now that you mention it, I did go to the Brick House Club just once, though. Later at home that night, I got a phone call about my dad being sick and I packed up everything and came back to Red Back."

"Oh, so you did hang out there?" Ms. Ella asks.

"Yep. But it was just that one time. Why do you ask?"

"Oh, just curious. Hey that one time you were there, did you have on a blue-and-white plaid shirt?

"Yeah, I did! You starting to sound like you were there, too! Did we meet?" he asks.

"Yeah, we met. Do you remember leaving the club with a pretty, short petite girl that night? You guys took a picture together in the club.

"Yeah! We did take a picture. She was fine! Things got pretty steamy with me and her in the back seat of my car that night in the parking lot. She was really a nice girl. I dropped her off at her house and it was late. She gave her number. I told her I'd call her the next day. When I got home that night I got a call that dad had just had a heart attack. So I threw everything I had into my car that night and headed to the hospital in Red Back. I couldn't find her number anywhere. I must have lost it when I was packing my stuff in such a hurry. Then I came back to New Orleans about a month later to handle some business. I couldn't remember where she stayed since it was dark and very late when I dropped her off at her house the night we met. Plus, I'd been drinking that night so my memory wasn't the best."

"Ray, that was my roommate Tammy. We grew up together and were best friends. She and I shared our deepest secrets. She was trying her best to find you and she never did."

"Well, where is she now? She's probably married. She was a really nice girl."

"She passed away by committing suicide."

"Suicide?" Ray was clearly shocked.

"Yes, Ray. She got pregnant that night and later had a baby. She kept trying to find you and she never did. It was hard on her because her parents didn't want her to have a baby out of wedlock so they never supported her. And she didn't want to give the baby away. When the baby was two months old, she committed suicide."

Rays face is starting to become flushed. He's finding it hard to finish chewing the food in his mouth.

"I didn't know. I didn't know." He says with a lump in his throat. "Where is the baby?"

"She's sitting right there." Ms. Ella says as she's nodding to Denise.

Denise has heard the entire conversation between Ms. Ella and Uncle Ray. She looks at Ray and her eyes start to swell as she's fighting to hold back tears. She's nervous. She doesn't know what his response is going to be. The question running through her mind is, "will he accept me or reject her?" Plus, she doesn't want to make a scene in front of the people she's just met.

Ray is looking at her with a dumbfounded look. His eyes start to swell with tears, too. He starts shaking his head and says, "I didn't know" under his breath. Then he says it again: "I didn't know!" But this time he says it out loud and his voice is cracking. He burst into tears and moves over to tightly hug and hold Denise who's finally decided that it's OK to let her tears flow, too.

The others at the house look at them embracing. No one knows what's going on except Ray, Ella and Denise.

Then Grandma asks out loud from the Lazy Boy chair she's sitting in, "Ray, baby, are you OK?"

"This is my daughter, Mamma! This is my daughter!"

"What!" Grandma replies. Aunt Earnestine and several others are in shock and tears.

"I didn't know anything about her," says Ray, still hugging Denise. "I didn't even know I had a daughter."

After hearing the loud commotion, Sidney and Lawrence move downstairs.

Sidney is taken aback by what he sees. He's known Uncle Ray his entire life. And while growing up, he'd never seen Uncle Ray shed a tear. He's always been this strong, witty, woman-chasing, macho man. He's never shown any sign of weakness or fear, not even in times of trouble like when another man in town was going around looking for him with a gun because he heard Ray was messing around with his wife. Ray just told everyone, "If he finds me, we'll handle it. But I'm not running from no man." That was the macho-ness of uncle Ray.

And now he's standing in Sidney's kitchen with tears in his eyes, asking for forgiveness.

"What's going on?" Sidney asks.

"This is my daughter. Your cousin! Come here man!" Uncle Ray says while looking straight at Josh.

Josh goes over to Ray and Denise and he's somewhat confused. "Baby, this is your grandfather." Denise tells him.

Uncle Ray reaches out to hug Josh and Denise at the same time.

There are very few dry eyes now as everyone sits back and takes this all in.

"I knew when I first met Josh in the driveway that there was something about him. A quick thought passed through my mind that said he looks just like my brother, Ray," Marcy says.

Karen, who's been sitting down the entire time with Ally standing next to her, tells her to give the tissue box in the living room to Denise and Ray.

Grandma gets up and walks over to the three and starts hugging and kissing Denise and Josh. Her new found granddaughter and great-grandson.

"See, didn't I tell you earlier that you're family?" she says, looking at Denise. "And look at my tall handsome great grand-son! Wow! I woke up with a great grand-daughter," she says while looking at Ally, "and I'm going to bed knowing I've got a great-grandson as well. I'm so proud!"

Grandpa also gets up to walk over to embrace and welcome the new family additions.

"Welcome to the family! I'm your granddad," he says looking at Denise, "and of course I'm your great-granddad!" he says, shaking Josh's hand and hugging him at the same time.

Marcy and Earnestine, who are both in tears as they meet their niece for the first time, follow suit.

"Welcome to the family, girl! I know you've already met us but now we're your aunts!" she says with tears in her eyes.

"And I guess that makes us your great-aunts." Marcy adds while looking at Josh.

Denise is completely overwhelmed with what's happening and she starts to cry on her Dad's shoulders. Her dad. The man she's wanted to find her entire life. She's finally found him.

Sidney walks over to Denise and says, "Welcome to the family! Can you believe we're first cousins?"

"I'm shocked, just like you," she says.

"And you too, man!" he says, beaming at Josh and shaking his hand. "You're my little cousin! That's probably why you were so good at golf so quickly!"

They both laugh.

Karen is happy to go over and hug Denise and welcome her. She's somewhat relieved that she won't have to worry about her messing around with Sidney.

"This is really crazy! But I'm glad it turned out like this. Welcome to the family!" she says, hugging Denise.

Denise looks at Karen and says, "Thank you. If you hadn't invited us over for Thanksgiving, this would have never happened. So … thank you again."

"You are more than welcome," Karen says, wiping tears from Denise's face.

As everyone continues to welcome and embrace Denise and Josh, Lawrence is trying out some of Denise's desserts. He's really admiring the presentation she has with her dishes.

Most people just make their cakes or pies and throw them on a plate and think nothing of the presentation. But not Denise. Her desserts have a certain type of decorative and professional presentation along with a homemade taste. That's what he wants in his restaurants. He's got to talk to her before the night is over about joining his company in a management position possibly over pastry and desserts at his restaurants.

Later on, after things have settled down after finding out this exciting news, everyone brings Denise and Josh up to speed with information about her family history. She's finding out about other relatives who live near and far but couldn't make it for Thanksgiving. Later, Denise is in the kitchen when she's approached by Lawrence.

"Well, congratulations on finding your family," he says.

"Thanks. Thank you. I'm still taking it all in," she replies while looking into Lawrence's dreamy eyes. Earlier, she put him on the back burner to find out if uncle Ray was her dad. And that worked out fine. Now she's got time for Lawrence.

"Family is always a good thing. It's very important to know your roots. So it's good you found them."

"Yeah, I know. So tell me about your restaurant."

"Well, we've been open for a few months now and we're doing great. We're actually going to open up two others shortly."

"Wow, congratulations on the success of them," Denise says.

"Well, look, I want to ask you something," he says.

"Yes. Yes. I will go out with you."

"What?" Lawrence says with surprise.

"Is that what you were going ask me? Please say yes just so I don't have egg on my face!" Denise says playfully.

"Well, no. I wanted ask you if you would consider being our head pastry chef … first. Then I was going ask you if you'd go out with me. So, you have egg just on one side of the face. Not your whole face."

They both laugh.

It's later in the night and everyone is getting ready to pack up and leave Sidney's house. Everyone's managed to exchange phone numbers with Denise so they can spend more time with her. On the way out the door, Uncle Ray walks with her, Ms. Ella and Josh.

"Now, Baby Girl, you be careful on the way home," he tells her. "You have enough gas?" He asks as he reaches into his pocket and pulls out money.

"I'm good, Ray. I'm good," she says.

"Well, take this anyway," Uncle Ray says as he forces the money on her. He's still happy about finding her and wants to do whatever he needs to do to make up for years he's missed with his daughter and his grandson.

"I'll be up this weekend and we'll go get lunch. OK?" he asks while hugging and simultaneously putting Josh in a head lock from behind.

"And Denise?"

"Yeah, Ray?"

"Call me Dad. OK?"

"OK ... Dad." Denise says with a grin and smile.

On her way driving back to the apartment, Ms. Ella has fallen asleep and Josh also has dozed off. As always, her motivational CD is playing. Denise is thinking about this exciting day she's had. She found her father, met a handsome guy and is going to get paid for something she loves to do. How her life has changed in one day.

"Your future is as bright as you can imagine it to be!" the man on the CD says.

Denise replies, "Yes, it is. Yes, it is."

ABOUT THE AUTHOR

Taurus King is an author, husband and father. He's an
entrepreneur and motivational speaker who encourages and
inspires people to live to their highest potential. He's also a
leader in both Mens Ministry and Childrens Ministry.